The Secret in the Stars

Nancy frowned. Dr. Stars's van was parked flush up against a metal guardrail. Slim as she was, there was no space to squeeze between the railing and the passenger side of the van. In order to see if he'd left a note on the front passenger side, Nancy would have to climb over the rail.

Cautiously, aware of the sheer drop a few feet away, Nancy clambered over the rail. The graveled area slanted downward toward the edge of the bluff.

Putting one hand on the van door to steady herself, Nancy stood on tiptoe and looked inside.

"That's strange," she murmured to herself. "The doors are locked, but the window on this side is open."

Suddenly the gravel crunched behind her. Nancy started to spin around, when a hand clamped down on her shoulder.

She staggered backward, the smooth soles of her sneakers slipping on loose stones, sending her skidding right toward the cliff's edge.

Nancy Drew
Mystery Stories

Available from Simon & Schuster

NANCY DREW® 156

THE SECRET IN THE STARS

CAROLYN KEENE

Aladdin Paperbacks
New York London Toronto Sydney Singapore

This book is a work of fiction. Any references to historical events, real people, or real locales are used fictitiously. Other names, characters, places, and incidents are the product of the author's imagination, and any resemblance to actual events or locales or persons, living or dead, is entirely coincidental.

First Aladdin Paperbacks edition August 2002
First Minstrel edition September 2000

ALADDIN PAPERBACKS
An imprint of Simon & Schuster
Children's Publishing Division
1230 Avenue of the Americas
New York, NY 10020

Printed in the United States of America

10 9 8 7 6 5 4 3

ISBN 0-671-04263-7

Contents

THE SECRET IN THE STARS

1

Shadow in the Woods

"What a perfect night for stargazing!" eighteen-year-old Nancy Drew remarked as she turned off the interstate at an exit marked River Heights State Park. Nancy had the top down on her Mustang convertible, and the breeze whipped through her reddish blond hair. Ned would love this, Nancy thought as she reached up to tuck a strand of hair back into her ponytail. She wished her boyfriend, Ned Nickerson, hadn't already gone back to Emerson College for the new semester.

It was nearly ten on a balmy mid-August Friday night. Nancy was driving her friends George Fayne and Bess Marvin to the park for a "star watch" party hosted by the famous radio personality Dr. Stars. As Nancy headed north on the narrow county road, the sky was already studded with thousands of stars.

"I'm so glad you found that flyer announcing Dr.

Stars being in town this weekend," she said to George.

"Me, too," George said from the front passenger seat. She raked her fingers through her short dark curls. "I missed his radio broadcast last weekend when I was hiking. I didn't even know he'd be in the area. This is a great chance to look through a serious top-of-the-line telescope."

"I haven't for ages," Nancy admitted. "We'll get to brush up on the constellations. On his broadcasts Dr. Stars makes you feel as though stargazing is the start of an adventure," Nancy added, glancing briefly at George, her blue eyes bright.

"Wrong!" Bess muttered from the backseat. "Feels like *boring!* At best."

Nancy bit back a smile. George and Bess were first cousins who not only looked completely unrelated—Bess was short and curvy with pale blond hair and huge blue eyes, while George was tall, athletic, and dark haired—but were as different as the sun and moon. Bess's idea of a good time was hitting the mall, shopping until she dropped, and topping the whole experience off with an ice-cream sundae, whereas George preferred playing basketball, racing on her in-line skates, or rock climbing.

"Bet you've never even heard of Dr. Stars or listened to his show on the radio," George said to her cousin. With that she switched on the car radio. "He's probably on right now," she remarked, checking the illuminated dial on her sports watch. She tuned the radio to a popular local talk-show station, then wrapped her arms around her long legs and settled back to listen.

"I thought he was supposed to be in the park," Bess commented.

"The program's probably taped ahead of time," Nancy pointed out, blinking in the glare of oncoming headlights. "Why are so many cars heading *back* to town?" she wondered. Before she could give the traffic another thought, a husky male voice with a pronounced Texas twang boomed out of the car speakers:

"This week's celestial happening is one of the big ones, sure to impress you whether you're an old hand at stargazing or about to take your first gander at the wonders of the night sky through a telescope. In just two nights fireworks—or should I say *starworks*—will explode above your head big time: the Perseid meteor shower. Until next time, this is Dr. Stars, wishing you night after glorious night of star hunting! And check my Dr. Stars Web page for listings of the upcoming stellar events—and for the next location of my Star Van tour. This week, River Heights. Next week— maybe *your* hometown!"

As strains of New Age electronic music rose above the announcer's sign-off, Nancy switched off the sound.

"What do you think Dr. Stars will look like?" Nancy asked. "It's hard to imagine the face that goes with that deep, twangy voice."

"Not for me," Bess remarked. "The guy sounds like he's ancient. Gray haired, pudgy, definitely short!"

"Oh, I don't know," George teased. "He could be tall and athletic with great biceps."

"Maybe," Bess conceded, "but don't you remember the guys in the astronomy club in high school? None

3

of them ever made me very interested in stargazing—at least not *this* kind."

"Ah, and what *other* kind of stargazing might you be interested in?" Nancy prodded, eyeballing Bess in the rearview mirror.

Bess's full lips drew up into a smile. "Right, like you have to ask. You know perfectly well that Will Ryder—my favorite movie star in the entire world—is supposed to be in town. I read it in *Exposé* when I was at the supermarket this morning."

Nancy shook her head. "Bess, you can't believe a word they write in those tabloids. None of it's true."

"Oh, some is," Bess insisted. "Last week's issue reported that Will was engaged to Isabel Ramos-Garcia, and then the announcement was on the regular TV news that night." Bess heaved a sigh. "That's one time I wish the tabloids had been wrong."

"Whatever," George said. "Just because Will Ryder *might* be in town doesn't mean you're going to run into him, Bess."

Bess hitched up the strap of her halter top. "Maybe, maybe not. But I'm sure he's more likely to be out dancing at a club like High Fives than hanging out at a state park with a bunch of astronomy freaks."

"Where there are sure to be lots of guys," Nancy pointed out. "It's a fact. More guys than girls go to these star parties—guys who aren't already engaged to a top Latina pop singer and actress. *Available* guys, Bess."

Bess stared out the window. "We'll be lucky if *any* guys are there tonight. How come all the cars are coming back toward town, and no one but us is headed for the park?"

Nancy frowned. "There should be some cars going our way. George, are you sure the flyer said the Star Van would be in the parking lot just inside the main entrance?"

George rummaged in the red backpack on the floor and pulled out a yellow flyer. She unfolded it as Nancy turned on the interior light. "Says right here— tonight's the first night of his visit to the River Heights area. He's setting up his telescope near his Star Van in the parking lot off this road, a quarter-mile inside the main entrance gate. We're on time, too," George said, checking her watch again. "It says any time after nine-thirty, with stargazing beginning at ten P.M. for 'early birds,'" she concluded with a chuckle. "One thing your club scene has in common with the astronomy crowd, Bess—you're all night crawlers."

"Watch it, Nancy!" Bess suddenly called out, gripping the back of Nancy's seat. "Look at those police lights!"

"I see," Nancy said, braking for the state trooper's car that straddled both lanes. Its blue and white warning lights spun on the roof, bathing the forest in an eerie glow.

"Do you think there's been an accident?" George wondered aloud.

Nancy peered past the police car and shook her head. "Looks more like a roadblock," she answered.

An officer approached and waved his flashlight at the convertible. At the sight of Nancy his expression brightened. "Nancy Drew!" he greeted her.

"Trooper Caruso." Nancy smiled back. She had met the officer before when she had been working on one of her cases. Nancy was well-known as a talented young detective. "What's happening?" she asked.

The officer tilted his hat back and nodded politely at George and Bess. "We've had to set up a roadblock. There's been a prowler reported on this side of the Woody Acres Estate. We're diverting all traffic while we search the area."

"We were headed for the park for Dr. Stars's sky watch tonight," George said, handing the officer the flyer. "Can we still get there?"

Officer Caruso nodded. "Sure—the park's not blocked off. You can make a U-turn and either head back to the interstate and take the first exit on the way back toward town. Or, if you know the back road through the park, you can take the first left onto Pinecrest, then another left into the park. Do you know your way to the parking lot from that entrance?" he asked Nancy.

"I do," Nancy assured him as she waved goodbye.

Nancy made her U-turn, then backtracked down the road. "Maybe this roadblock explains some of the traffic heading toward town. People aren't familiar with the back entrance to the park."

Several miles later Nancy turned off the two-lane park drive onto a smaller one-lane blacktop. It was a moonless night; leafy trees arched over the road, blocking the starlight. Except for the narrow beam of light cast by Nancy's headlights, the road was pitch-black.

"Are you *sure* you know where you're going?" Bess asked, leaning forward. Peering into the dark tangle of brush and trees, she shuddered. "Like, shouldn't there be a sign or something?"

"Not from this end," George pointed out. "Except for some rental cabins, this part of the park is pretty rugged and undeveloped."

"We're still a couple of miles from the main gate," Nancy interjected, then caught her breath. Out of the corner of her eye she saw something darker than the surrounding shadows dart upright through the dense shrubbery into the trees.

Before Nancy could draw her next breath, the shape had vanished, blending into the deep leafy darkness of the forest. "What was that?" she cried, just as Bess shrieked, "Did you see it? It looked like a bear!" Bess pointed off to the left where the shadowy form had vanished from the side of the road.

Nancy slowed down a little. "A bear?" She shook her head. "No way, Bess. This is River Heights, not Yellowstone."

"Bess might be right," George interjected. "Last time I was here one of the rangers said black bears are coming back to the area. They've spotted one around the park. Once or twice maybe—they're pretty rare. Actually, I'd love to see one."

"Have you lost it or what?" Bess demanded. "I didn't come here for a bear-watch. Bears eat people—at least in all the stories you read. Let's just get out of here, Nancy. I mean, do you really think it's a good idea to hang around while something deadly lurks in the bushes?"

"Something—or someone," Nancy said, thinking of the prowler. She knew Bess was right, and yet she couldn't help being intrigued by the possibility of a

7

mystery. She was tempted to stop the car and investigate.

Before Nancy could say another word, a deer bounded out of the bushes to the left, dashing across the road right in front of the car. Jamming on the brakes, she swerved onto the shoulder. The car jerked to a halt.

"A deer," Bess gasped in relief. "It was just a deer."

"Is it all right?" George asked, anxiously staring at the shoulder of the road. There was the sound of something breaking through the brush. Then silence. "Too dark to see anything—but I think I heard it."

"George, I'm sure I didn't hit it. It was able to run," Nancy reassured her friend. But Nancy couldn't take her eyes off the thicket to her left. The deer had bolted from the woods seconds before, but she was sure—or *almost* sure—she'd just heard something rustling through the leaves. Another animal, she told herself. But something inside her wondered if it was the two-legged kind.

Nancy put the thought out of her mind, took a deep breath, and pulled back onto the road.

A few minutes later they approached the main parking area. A sign at the entrance read Day Use Only, but the iron gate was open, and as Nancy steered through the gate, her headlights illuminated one of Dr. Stars's yellow flyers fluttering from the gatepost. Lampposts bordered the lot, but the lights were out.

"Weird!" George exclaimed as Nancy drove past the open-sided shed that sheltered a park map and visitor information. "No one's here."

"No one but Dr. Stars," Nancy said, motioning toward the far end of the lot where a full-size van was parked. As Nancy drew closer her headlights illuminated the area around the van. A raccoon rooting in a trash can looked up startled, its eyes huge in the glare of Nancy's lights. For a moment it remained frozen, then bolted into the tall clumps of goldenrod and weeds in the meadow beyond the parking lot.

Nancy noticed that a few camp chairs had been set up around a long metal portable table. "I don't understand where everyone is," she said, pulling into a space near the van. She grabbed a flashlight from the glove compartment, shouldered her bag, then pocketed her keys. She got out of the car and George followed.

"Just as I predicted—some party!" Bess complained, climbing out, too.

Outside the car Nancy tugged down the legs of her slim black cropped pants and tucked in her sleeveless white blouse, then made her way toward the van. Her cobalt blue canvas sneakers muffled the sound of her steps as she walked.

She turned on her flashlight to check out the display set up on the table. A black cloth covered the surface. Stacks of handouts, flyers, and star maps were arranged neatly along one edge, each stack held down by a small rock. Nancy directed her light toward the far end of the display: a poster was propped up on a portable easel. The poster featured a cartoon-like drawing of a chubby astronomer peering comically through a telescope at the sky. Right above him the Big Dipper was tilted at a weird angle and looked as if it was dripping milk on top of his bald head.

Slowly sweeping the area with her flashlight, Nancy

wondered why wide black electrical tape covered the metal parts of all the camp chairs.

"I don't get it," George said, walking up. She hooked her hands in the back pockets of her jeans and surveyed the deserted lot. "The star watch has to be on for tonight or he wouldn't have all this stuff set up."

"Maybe Dr. Stars took everyone out for a hike, to get a better view or something," Bess suggested. "Maybe we're too late and should head back to the car, Nancy. And just in case you guys are going to start tramping off looking for him, I'm not dressed for a hike." Bess chafed her bare arms. "Besides, it's cool up here." She was wearing white shorts, a halter top and platform sandals. She stepped closer to George and Nancy, and looked nervously over her shoulder. "And remember the bears."

"Something's wrong here," Nancy said quietly, ignoring Bess's pleas. Dr. Stars had gone to a lot of trouble to set up for this night's stargazing lecture, but no one had come. And to all appearances the astronomer himself had walked out on his own party. Nancy couldn't shake the feeling that something strange had happened. She decided to check the van. "Let's see if Dr. Stars fell asleep or something," Nancy said, making for the corner of the parking area.

"Don't leave us behind—in the dark!" Bess cried, hurrying after Nancy, George at her side.

Dr. Stars had parked the van close to the guardrail at the edge of the lot. This end of the parking area butted against forest on one side with a small sign marking the head of a hiking trail. Two Dumpsters with animal-proof latches were just to the right of the trail head. On the other side of the van, beyond the guardrail, if Nancy remembered correctly, the area bordered a steep cliff. Nancy couldn't see it in the dark, but she knew the river ran through the valley below—right through the Woody Acres Estate. Nancy looked over the guardrail and saw the lights from the main house on the estate grounds. From where she stood she couldn't see the main road or lights from the trooper's car, if he still had the road blocked. Maybe the prowler had been caught, but if not, he might still be lurking in the area.

No point jumping to conclusions, she told herself. Why would someone prowling around Woody Acres Estate want to hurt an astronomer? Or have anything to do with the mystery of where the stargazers had gone?

Nancy turned back to the van, slowly scanning first the driver's side, then the back of the vehicle with her flashlight. It appeared to be painted deep blue, with Dr. Stars's cartoon logo on one side. Curtains were drawn across the side and back windows. Nancy tried the back and side doors, but they were locked. Nancy knocked on the rear door. "Dr. Stars?" she called out. "He's not here," Nancy told her friends.

"Maybe he left a note or something on the table," George suggested. "I'll go and check. I've got a penlight on my key chain."

While George and Bess headed back for the table, Nancy went to check the front of the van. She aimed her flashlight through the front window on the driver's side. On the seat she spied a couple of road maps, an open notebook, and an open coffee thermos in the cup holder.

11

"He sure left in a hurry," she called back to George and Bess.

Nancy frowned. The van was parked flush up against the metal guardrail. Slim as she was, there was no space to squeeze between the railing and the passenger side of the van. To look in the window on the front passenger side, Nancy would have to climb over the rail. Cautiously, aware of the sheer drop a few feet away, Nancy clambered over the rail. The graveled area slanted downward toward the edge of the bluff. Clumps of tall weeds sprouted out of the stones and scratched at Nancy's bare calves and ankles. The footing was tricky, and Nancy kept her eye away from the edge of the cliff and on the van. Putting one hand on the door to steady herself, Nancy stood on tiptoe and looked inside.

"That's strange," she murmured to herself. "The doors are locked but the window on this side is open." Nancy reached through the window to pull up the door lock.

Suddenly the gravel crunched behind her. Nancy started to spin around, when a hand clamped down on her shoulder. She staggered backward, the smooth soles of her sneakers slipping on the loose stones, sending her skidding toward the cliff's edge.

2

Who Are You?

Nancy's scream echoed across the parking lot.

"Nancy! Are you okay?" George cried out from over by the table.

Nancy couldn't find her voice. As she struggled to regain her balance, the hand on her shoulder tightened its grip. Nancy tried to squirm away without losing her footing, and for a moment she teetered precariously on the edge of the cliff.

Nancy heard the thump of George's running shoes against the macadam surface. "Hey, let go of her!" George yelled, running up just as Nancy found herself being pushed back toward the guardrail and safety.

"If I do," a gruff male voice declared, "she'll fall." The man waited until Nancy had climbed over the guardrail, then loosened his hold on her. "You were about to knock over that telescope," he offered by way of explanation. "I had to stop you."

Furious, Nancy glared up at the owner of the voice, but she could barely make out his face in the dark. Her flashlight had landed a few feet away in the weeds. Its lamp was out, the bulb probably broken. What telescope? she wondered as her pulse slowed down to normal. Still the man had no right to grab her like that.

"You could have killed me," Nancy told him hotly. Her shoulder hurt where he'd grabbed her.

"More like I saved you," he said, pulling out a small flashlight and flicking it on. Nancy noted it had a red filter covering the glass and an unusually narrow beam. The light it cast was very dim, but it was enough to illuminate the guy's face. He was a trim, athletic-looking man about her dad's age with salt-and-pepper hair and piercing deep-set eyes. He didn't flinch from her gaze and fairly snapped at her, "Besides, why are you snooping around here—and where is everybody, anyway?"

Nancy couldn't believe it. The guy actually sounded as if he suspected she had something to do with the crowd's disappearance.

"You have some nerve asking that," Bess spoke up, gently massaging Nancy's shoulder. "Did he hurt you?" she asked.

"I'm okay," Nancy assured Bess. She checked to her right. Sure enough, a telescope was perched on the wrong side of the guardrail, directed down toward the valley below. A single misstep and she might have knocked the scope over. She should have seen it but had been too busy watching her footing when she looked in the van. Why did Dr. Stars set it up in such a crazy place?

14

"I didn't see the scope," Nancy admitted. "It's sure not safe where you put it, though . . ."

"Where *I* put it?" The man let out a low, gruff laugh. "I'm not that stupid."

"Look, Dr. Stars . . ." George exclaimed with annoyance. "First, you nearly kill our friend to save your telescope, and now—"

The man cleared his throat noisily, cutting George off. "Dr. Stars?" He laughed another unpleasant laugh. "You think *I'm* Dr. Stars?"

"Aren't you?" Nancy and Bess asked in unison.

"Fortunately—not." The man shrugged. "I came to check out his star-watch lecture. Looks like a nonevent to me," he remarked, sounding almost gleeful. He walked around the far side of the van, and the girls followed him.

"Well, if you're not Dr. Stars, who are you? And where is Dr. Stars?" Nancy asked.

The man shrugged. "Beats me. I'm Derek Randall," he informed Nancy brusquely. "I'm a professor of astronomy at Grimsley College, outside L.A."

Nancy frowned slightly. She had read something about Grimsley recently. But where? And about what?

"So why are you bothering to come to an amateur astronomy lecture?" George asked as Derek Randall ambled over to the display table and pursed his lips at the sight of Dr. Stars's cartoon poster.

"I came across one of his flyers at the north campground this afternoon. Seemed this star party was a perfect chance to put a *real* face to the name," he said, gesturing toward the drawing of the radio personality. "I've been subjected to hearing his dumb show for years."

"You've never met him?" Nancy asked.

"Believe me, we don't travel in the same circles, though Bob Steller—that's your Dr. Stars's real name, by the way—and I have crossed paths—or maybe swords—in the astronomy journals. He scooped me a few years back. We both spotted a new comet at the same time, but he managed to report the discovery two hours before I did. Or at least that's what the official log of the Astronomical Society reported. I'm convinced he pulled some strings. Now it's known as Steller's Comet, not Randall's," Derek said bitterly.

"People who discover comets get them named after themselves?" Bess sounded impressed.

"Sure, like Comet Hale-Bopp or Halley's Comet," Derek explained. "Anyway, Steller got sole credit for a discovery we should have shared. Can't say that endeared him to me," Derek admitted. "I'm not one of his fans."

"Well, I sure am," George said, defending Dr. Stars. "I think he's doing a good thing with this Star Van."

Derek nodded quickly. "I won't argue with that. His campaign to get people interested in astronomy is good. But like everything else the guy's involved in, this is just one more way for him to promote himself—*his* career. The only star he really cares about is himself."

And are you any different? Nancy wondered.

Derek shoved his fists in his pockets and glanced around the still-deserted lot. "This time his fans seem to have let him down."

Nancy picked up a glossy photo lying behind the poster.

"Weird," Derek said, peering over her shoulder, illuminating the picture with his flashlight. "I thought he'd be more my age."

Nancy, Bess, and George all looked at the handsome face smiling back at them from the black-and-white photo. Dr. Stars was in his late twenties with a charming smile, dimples in his chin, and mischievous light eyes.

"He sure looks younger than he sounds on the radio," Nancy commented.

"And better looking, too," Bess remarked. "But why would he choose such a nerdy cartoon of himself for his flyer and poster? The guy's gorgeous, but this makes him look like a forty-something geek."

Derek casually shrugged his shoulders. "Go figure. The guy is weird, and his poster is very unprofessional. I've got to get going. Do you girls have another flashlight? I think yours bit the dust back there."

"In my trunk," Nancy said tightly. Derek Randall was beyond stuffy, and arrogant.

"I'll walk you back to your car," Derek volunteered, gesturing with his small flashlight.

"No need," Nancy told him. The man was truly maddening. First he practically knocked her over a cliff, and now he was all politeness and concern.

"Whatever," Derek said. "Good luck tracking down Dr. Stars. He sure has a pretty weird sense of how to set up a telescope! I don't know what he was thinking," Derek grumbled, heading over to the railing. "But it's just dumb luck you didn't knock it over," he shot at Nancy. With that, Derek carefully lifted the telescope over the guardrail and put it on the asphalt. "This way the next gust of wind—or next person snooping around the van—will have a harder time knocking it over."

"I'm not sure you should have moved that," Bess remarked.

"Just doing a fellow stargazer a good turn." Derek shrugged and retreated to the trail, vanishing quickly around the bend and into the forest.

Nancy watched the dark swallow him up and shook her head. "Good night to you, too," she said, feeling irritated. Derek Randall was arrogant, surly, and generally unpleasant. Still, he *was* right to move the scope. Nancy shuddered to think she'd almost knocked that expensive piece of equipment over a cliff.

"I don't like that man," George said, voicing Nancy's opinion of the astronomer. She touched Nancy's arm. "Let's get going. There's no action around here."

"And the club scene is just heating up," Bess reminded them, a hopeful note in her voice.

"In a minute, Bess. I'm game for some dancing myself, but first I want to check something out." Nancy started back toward the van, pausing to look down the trail. Her eyes were getting used to the dark, and she could see that the path into the woods was empty. Derek had headed back toward the north campgrounds.

"You think he's still lurking around?" George whispered.

"I don't know. I want to check out some stuff I saw on the front seat of the van. I can't believe Dr. Stars

18

would plan a star-watch evening, set up a table, then disappear."

"All the van's doors are locked, but I noticed before that the window on the front passenger side was open. I was about to pop the lock when Derek grabbed me. Let me borrow your penlight."

"Nancy, you'd better be careful. The footing is pretty tricky," George warned, handing over the light.

"Tell me about it! I've learned my lesson." Carefully Nancy climbed over the guardrail and within seconds had unlocked the van's front door. She cracked it open, and by sucking in her breath, she was able to squeeze into the front seat. She unlatched the driver's door from inside the van. The interior light went on. Then she picked up the notebook on the front seat. It had a sturdy black cover and a black plastic spiral binding.

"It's some kind of diary," she told her friends as she scanned the journal. The entries were made in a neat, precise hand. As she read them to herself she began to smile. Each entry was dated with the time, date, location, and sky conditions. Dr. Stars's notes were beautifully written, like little poems: each one described the environment where Dr. Stars had set up his telescope, what flowers were in bloom, the color of the sunset while he waited for dark. On almost every other page he'd sketched and labeled constellations. Next to each was a drawing: Ursa Major, Nancy knew meant the Great Bear, which was another name for the Big Dipper—instead of a sketch of a soup ladle Dr. Stars had sketched a chubby cartoon bear; Cygnus was next to a drawing of a swan; Boötes was next to a comical rendering of a couple of cows.

To Nancy's delight and surprise, skillful drawings of birds and flowers and even a couple of squirrels filled some of the margins. Realistic drawings alternated with cartoon renderings of people, animals, plants. Dr. Stars loved to draw, that was obvious.

Nancy flipped through the diary, then frowned. "Look, this makes no sense," she said. She held the book so George could look at it.

"He started a diary entry this evening at six but never got further than talking about the best location to set up his telescope. The entry stops midsentence. It looks as if the next page was torn out." Nancy showed George the place where bits of paper still clung to the black plastic spiral binding. Puzzled, Nancy studied the book a moment longer, then clambered out of the driver's side, put the notebook back on the front seat exactly as she'd found it, and slammed the door behind her, locking it.

As she crossed the lot back toward her car, she heaved a sigh. "Hey, guys," she said, worried. "I just can't shake the feeling that something has happened to Dr. Stars."

3

A Voice in the Dark

"Did I hear my name?" A male voice with a distinctive Texas twang called from behind them.

Nancy turned abruptly and was blinded by the glare of a camper's lantern. Quickly she shielded her eyes and averted her gaze. The man lowered his lantern so the light was cast on the ground, not on Nancy's face. Her vision recovered quickly, and Nancy found herself staring at the real-life version of the glossy promo photo of Dr. Stars. In person, with his piercing blue eyes, a mop of unruly blond hair, and standing about six feet tall, Dr. Stars was even cuter than his picture. He wore jeans and a lightweight khaki vest over his T-shirt.

"You're Dr. Stars!" Bess gasped. "We were *so* worried."

"Especially with that prowler lurking around Woody Acres," George added. "The state troopers detoured all traffic away from the main entrance to the park."

"Prowler?" Dr. Stars asked. "State troopers? Around here?" He glanced protectively toward his van.

"Not exactly," Nancy hurried to assure him. "As far as we know the prowler was seen only at Woody Acres—that's a big estate that borders the park. You can see it from the overlook where your van is parked."

Dr. Stars breathed a sigh of relief. "Any would-be thief staking out an estate probably wouldn't be interested in my gear. Who does this Forest Acres belong to?"

"*Woody* Acres," Nancy corrected him with a smile. "Carlos Ramos—his grandfather made a fortune years ago in the importing business. The family's had the estate since the early fifties. But you probably know Carlos Ramos better as the head of Hot Sauce, the big new Latin and fusion music record label."

"He's positively rolling in platinum records," Bess supplied. "Three of his artists won Grammys this year."

Dr. Stars lifted his shoulders. "Guess I'm a little out of the music scene. Can't say I've ever heard of either Hot Sauce Records or Carlos Ramos."

"When you weren't here, we began to worry," Nancy went on.

"Worried?" Dr. Stars repeated, glancing hurriedly from the van to the display table to his poster. Slowly a sheepish grin spread across his handsome, boyish face, and he put down the lantern, which threw off a welcome circle of light.

"Sorry you girls got upset. You must have wondered, 'Was everyone abducted by aliens or what?'"

He chuckled but then his voice grew serious. "I'm surprised they didn't tell you at the main gate."

"Tell us what?" Nancy asked.

"That the flyer—*this* flyer"—he tapped the stack of yellow flyers on the table—"had a typo. Wrong date."

"But then why did you bother to set up?" George wondered.

"Oh, this is left over from this afternoon." Dr. Stars gestured breezily toward the display. "Kids from some of the campsites came over. I told them a bit about astronomy, suggested they come back tomorrow night for stargazing, passed out my flyers—that's when we saw the date was wrong," he added. "Didn't you see the note I left, um, somewhere around here?" He riffled through the material on the table. "Or did I tape it to the back of the van?"

"No," Nancy told him. "I looked around the van. I hope you don't mind," she added quickly, "but it was so strange that no one was here, that I even checked inside. I found your journal but no note."

"Maybe it blew away," Bess suggested.

"Or maybe it's still in your pocket." Nancy laughed, pointing to the top pocket of the astronomer's vest.

Dr. Stars peered down into his pocket and fished out a piece of yellow lined paper with frayed edges. "Do you believe it? I forgot to post the note." He made a small sound of self-disgust and gave an embarrassed shrug. "At least I remembered my camera bag," he said. "I admit it. I'm a bit of the absentminded professor."

"Speaking of professors," Nancy said, "did you run into your old pal back there on the trail?" It had been only a few minutes from when Derek headed up the trail, and Dr. Stars had emerged from the trailhead.

"My pal?" Dr. Stars frowned. "Who do you mean?"

"Derek Randall, who teaches at Grimsley," Nancy supplied. "Of course you wouldn't have recognized him, I guess, since you haven't ever met. Still, he should have said hello to you. He'd just seen your photo."

"Where?"

"Here," George answered. "He came looking for you and told us all about your rivalry. Can't say you missed much if you didn't see him."

Dr. Stars pursed his lips. Shaking his head ruefully, he remarked, "Oh, *that* Derek Randall. Well, you're right about that. I don't need trouble—or rivals snooping around here now. Things can get pretty strange in astronomy circles, but as I said, I didn't run into anyone back on the trail." He paused, then cocked his head and eyed Nancy. "Don't think I ever got your name, or your friends' for that matter. I'm Bob Steller and you are . . ."

"Nancy Drew." Nancy shook his hand, which was callused. "These are my friends Bess Marvin and her cousin, George Fayne."

"Are you visiting the area?" Dr. Stars asked.

"No. We live right here in River Heights," Bess told him. "But when we saw the flyer—"

George cleared her throat loudly. "*We?*" Bess kicked George's foot. George ignored the jab and continued. "Anyway, we're big fans of your show, and when I heard you were in town, I thought it'd be cool to check out your star lectures."

"Actually," Nancy added, "since we're here and it's

still pretty clear out, could we look through your tele-scope?"

Dr. Stars hesitated only a second, then shrugged. "Why not? It'll make up for all that worry I put you through." As he spoke, a light breeze swept across the parking lot. "Maybe I should pack this stuff up first," he said, pulling a plastic milk crate from under the table.

"We'll help," Bess volunteered. "If that's okay?" She flashed a pretty smile at Dr. Stars.

"Be my guests," he said, carefully stacking the handouts. With Bess's help he folded the black table-cloth, then tucked it in a corner of the crate.

"How come you use a black cloth?" Nancy asked as Dr. Stars shoved the crate under the table.

"Black doesn't show dirt easily—I'm on the road a lot—and a tablecloth keeps the handouts clean," he replied, dusting off his hands. "So let's do some stargazing," he announced cheerfully.

"I can't wait!" Bess said, hurrying to keep up with the astronomer.

Nancy and George exchanged a knowing glance. Seeing Dr. Stars, Bess had transformed her boredom with stargazing into a consuming passion. Thinking about the way Bob Steller sounded on the radio, Nancy wondered aloud, "You know, Dr. Stars, you sound different in person."

"I do?" he said, his twang deep as ever.

"You do. Your voice sounds huskier on the air," Nancy pointed out.

"I went to a voice doctor. Chronic laryngitis," Dr. Stars explained as they approached the van. He rubbed his throat. "Glad to hear all his treatments

25

helped. I've also been working with a voice therapist. But the shows through the next couple of weeks were taped a while back, before I had my treatments."

"I would have recognized your voice *anywhere,*" Bess declared passionately.

"Give me a break!" George murmured, lifting her eyebrows.

Dr. Stars seemed flattered. "Well, Ms. Bess Marvin, you can't imagine how happy I am to hear that."

As Dr. Stars approached the telescope, he frowned. "Did you girls move this?" he asked.

"No, but Derek Randall did," George informed him.

"He was afraid it might get knocked over the cliff. In fact," Nancy admitted ruefully, "I almost did knock it over when I tried to look into your van to see if I could figure out what happened to you."

"So my rival actually did me a favor?" Dr. Stars sounded skeptical. "Not at all in character—from what I've heard about him."

Nancy shook her head firmly. "Maybe not. Still, I got the impression he really does care about astronomy as much as you do. The telescope was so close to the edge of the cliff on the other side of the guardrail, and it was pointed toward the ground—"

"It was *what?*" Dr. Stars was astounded. "I set it up this afternoon for the kids, to demonstrate how to use a telescope. I put it on a level spot on the pavement on *this* side of the guardrail. Believe me, I didn't want any kid falling over a cliff!" he declared hotly. Raking his fingers through his messy blond hair, he looked helplessly at Nancy. "Someone must have moved it."

"But why?" Nancy wondered, leaning over the

guardrail. In the dark only the lights from the main house on Woody Acres were visible, though during the day a person might be able to see the road from here. "Unless it was the prowler trying to scope out the estate before he went down there," Nancy suggested doubtfully.

"Well, let's not worry about it now. The telescope is safe, and you girls want to look through it." Dr. Stars adjusted the legs on the tripod that supported the telescope so that it stood level and was at an appropriate height for the girls to look through. After turning a couple of big knobs, he swiveled the scope so that it pointed up toward the darkest part of the sky. He then checked the eyepiece, adjusted the angle of the scope, and peered through it. "Focus is off," he mumbled. Keeping his gaze on the sky, he felt around the side of the scope. "Now, where is that focus ring? The knob on the ring is missing."

Nancy, Bess, and George studied the side of the scope. Sure enough, a short metal screw was protruding from the black metal body of the scope. But the small knob that should have been attached to it was gone.

"What could have happened to it?" Dr. Stars asked, dismayed. He picked up the lantern and held it high to illuminate the area around the telescope.

"Maybe it fell off when Derek moved it," Bess suggested.

"If it did, we'll never find it at night in the dark." Nancy sighed. "You'd better wait until morning. Still, telescopes are meant to be moved around. It seems strange that it would fall off like that."

"*If* it fell off!" Dr. Stars said ominously.

"What do you mean?" George asked.

Nancy felt a sudden chill. "I think I know what Dr. Stars is thinking."

"You said Derek Randall was the last person to touch the scope," Dr. Stars reminded Nancy.

"Yes, but I don't see how he had time to take off a knob. It took just moments to move it," Nancy mused, sure she would have noticed if Randall had been fiddling with the telescope.

"Who else would bother to steal a focusing knob? And why?" George asked.

"We're not sure anyone stole it," Nancy pointed out. "If someone moved the telescope and was careless, the knob might have dropped off and be lost over the cliff. On the other hand," Nancy added in a serious tone, "someone could have vandalized the telescope. Someone who thought Dr. Stars's lecture was tonight and wanted to sabotage it."

4

A Closer Look

The next afternoon Nancy parked her Mustang in the public lot off South Street in River Heights' revitalized waterfront district and checked her watch: It was one-ten. Good. She had twenty minutes before she was to meet Bess for ice cream, more than enough time to visit Star Wares, the downtown astronomy and science store. Nancy fed the meter, then crossed the street under a pure blue sky. The August sun was pleasantly warm on her shoulders, and her short flippy skirt fluttered in a gentle river breeze.

The info from Dr. Stars's handouts had piqued her curiosity about stargazing, and she wanted to prep herself to get the most out of his talk at the park that night. Meanwhile, a visit to the shop would give her a chance to check out telescopes firsthand. She'd been puzzling over the incidents of the night before. How easily could someone remove a focusing knob—or how likely was one to drop off?

Only a block from where Nancy had parked, the storefront was one of the largest in the area. Though it had been open for almost a year, Nancy had never been inside. White stars, yellow crescent moons, and ringed planets decorated the blue awning shading the store windows. Nancy hitched up the thin straps of her turquoise T-shirt and strode out of the bright sun into the shop.

When Nancy's eyes adjusted to the subdued interior lighting, she took in the floor-to-ceiling wooden bookshelves, posters, maps of the heavens, and display tables holding globes of all sizes.

The cash register and a computer terminal sat on a long glass-front display case situated in a corner of the room. Behind the counter, an arched doorway opened into a second room filled with telescopes and all sorts of stargazing paraphernalia.

"Need help?" the clerk sitting behind the cash register asked. He was a lanky college-age guy with a friendly smile and wire-rimmed glasses.

Nancy returned his grin. "You bet. I want something to get me started on stargazing. Something readable but with lots of information."

The clerk handed her a thick paperback. "This is a guide to backyard astronomy. It's pretty thorough but easy to understand. It even has a lot about meteor showers. I guess you know the Perseids begins tonight—though the peak isn't until tomorrow night." He glanced around the store and shrugged. "Why don't you look this book over, while I check the stockroom. We've been out of the other really terrific intro to astronomy, but we just got a big shipment from our wholesaler. Maybe it's waiting to be unpacked."

"Great!" Nancy told him. "No hurry, I'll browse through this, and I wanted to look at the telescopes if that's okay."

"Be my guest," the cashier told her, locking the register.

As he went back to the stockroom, Nancy set the book near the register, then passed through the arched door into the back of the shop. She took a quick look around, faced with a bewildering array of telescopes—some small enough to fit in a large backpack, others a good foot in diameter, and each perched on its own tripod. A sign encouraged "experienced viewers" to handle the scopes but warned newcomers to ask for help.

Nancy checked to see if she could spot a telescope that was similar to Dr. Stars's. In the confusion of the night before she had forgotten to notice the brand name. The telescopes closest to her were smaller than Dr. Stars's. As she surveyed the display looking for a more sophisticated model, she was startled to see she wasn't alone.

A tall well-built man was examining a medium-size scope. His back was toward Nancy, but as he straightened up, she saw his profile. Nancy recognized him instantly. Derek Randall! As Nancy debated whether she even wanted to approach him, she saw him unscrew a small knob on the telescope, study it, then turn to face her.

"I had a feeling I was being watched," he said, his

features registering surprise. "We have to stop meeting this way, Ms.—" he joked, sounding nervous.
"Come to think of it, I never did get your name."

Nancy watched as he fumbled to screw the knob
back on the telescope. "It's Nancy Drew, and what exactly are you doing to that telescope?"

"Not knocking it over a cliff, Ms. Drew," he shot
back. He approached Nancy, his hands in his pockets.

Nancy rolled her eyes but refused to be put off.
"Dr. Stars's scope was missing its focusing knob last
night."

"Very observant." Derek's eyes narrowed, and he
regarded her coldly. "And when exactly did you notice
that?"

"When did you?" Nancy countered, tossing her hair
back.

Derek cleared his throat. "When I moved it from
where that idiot had set it up."

"But he didn't set it up there," Nancy informed the
astronomer.

"Then who did?"

"Someone who wanted it to fall over the cliff."

Derek shrugged. "That same someone could have
pushed it over the edge just as easily," he pointed out.
"But I gather since you *know* Bob Steller had set it up
elsewhere, you must have finally met the man himself—which means he actually turned up."

"Yes, he did," Nancy was pleased to point out. "And
he's a pretty nice guy." Unlike you! she added to herself.

Derek shrugged. "And what was his excuse?"

"For what?" Nancy asked.

"For standing up his fans—and the rest of us," Derek said, leaning with one hand against the wall.

"Wrong date on the flyer. Apparently he was off at the main entrance gate, informing the park rangers." Nancy paused, trying to see past Derek's seemingly casual air. "It was an honest mistake, although he does seem a little spacey," she concluded.

"Like I told you, the guy's all front. He's just out for a buck and self-promotion." Derek lifted his shoulders and sighed. "Beats me, though, how he got this successful. I always had him figured for a wily, careful businessman—not the sort to make mistakes on flyers." He shrugged again and started for the front of the store.

At that moment the clerk hurried into the room, his head down, almost butting Derek in the chest. "Sorry!" the clerk apologized. He was holding a book in one hand.

Recognizing Derek, the clerk asked. "Did you find the model you were looking for?" He gestured toward the display.

"I did, and thanks," Derek said, continuing toward the exit.

"If you're really into stargazing, Dr. Stars is giving a lecture tonight in the park," the clerk offered. "He's worth checking out."

"So I've heard," Derek said in a bored tone. "Think I'll pass on that this time around." With a small nod at Nancy, he left the store.

"You don't know what you're missing," the clerk said under his breath. Meeting Nancy's eyes, he shrugged sheepishly. "Some of these purely academic types—they are *so* not into fun."

"You know him?" Nancy asked. She wanted to hear the clerk's opinion of the man.

"Not by name, just spotted him for what he is—an astronomer. I'm sure he is by the questions he was asking. But I knew he'd be down on Dr. Stars right from the get-go. Some of the purists in the field hate anyone's commercial success. You can imagine what the ivory tower crowd thinks of Bob Steller and his radio show."

Nancy said nothing. If the clerk didn't know Derek Randall by name, Nancy wasn't about to tell him he was Dr. Stars's chief rival. That reminded Nancy why she'd come to the shop. "I'm sorry, I never got to look at the telescopes," she confessed. "Could you explain how they focus?"

"No problemo," the clerk said. "Demonstrations are the fun part of this job." With that he gave Nancy a tour of the different kinds of telescopes. He explained that different scopes had different focusing devices: some were glued to the scope; some had Phillips screws; others had nylon hand-twist screws— and a few had knobs like the ones on Dr. Stars's telescope. Nancy filed away all these facts in her head but felt frustrated. Checking out the focusing knobs in the store proved only that someone had either deliberately taken the knob or loosened it—or the knob could have just fallen off.

Nancy followed the clerk back to the register. "This book on backyard astronomy looks the most useful," she said, digging in her backpack for her wallet. "I'll take it. It looks like a good introduction."

The clerk gave her a thumbs-up. "Good choice. An even better introduction are star parties," he added, handing Nancy her change.

"I imagine those have nothing to do with Hollywood," Nancy joked.

"No way! The local astronomy club sponsors them, at least once a month—sometimes more often in good weather. You should take one in sometime. It's laid-back and fun. Anyone with a decent telescope sets it up, and everyone's welcome to join in. Can't think of a better intro to astronomy and the local crowd." The clerk rummaged in a drawer beneath the counter.

"Here, take this," he said, handing Nancy a bright blue flyer. "The River Heights Astronomy Club is hosting a party tomorrow night up at the state park. And by the way, my name's Richard."

"I'm Nancy. Will you be there?" she asked, thinking that George wasn't dating anyone special, and that Richard might just be George's type.

"You bet. I put together the RHAC newsletter. Unfortunately this issue's going to be thin on visuals. My camera funked out on me. Usually I take pictures at these events."

"Hey, I've got an idea. If I can make it, I'll bring my camera. I'm a pretty mean photographer," she told him. "Will you be at Dr. Stars's lecture tonight?"

Richard shook his head. "Can't. We're open late tonight, and the manager asked me to pull a double," he said, making a sad face. Then he brightened. "But see you tomorrow."

"Sure," Nancy said, knowing she could convince

George to spend a third night stargazing. And maybe the very idea of a party would lure Bess back up to the park.

At the thought of Bess, Nancy winced. A quick glance at her watch proved she was a good ten minutes late for her ice-cream date. She said goodbye to Richard and hurried out. Fortunately she was only two blocks from Sweety Pies, the ice-cream parlor and bakery that overlooked the river. Clutching her Star Wares bag, Nancy half-jogged down the block, then made a left onto River Street, hurrying toward the row of two-story buildings fronting the river.

Nancy crossed River Street and headed for Sweety Pies. As she stepped off the curb to cross a narrow alleyway, she heard someone gun an engine. All at once a motorcycle careened out of the alley, heading straight toward her. Nancy jumped back on the sidewalk, the cycle missing her by inches.

"Hey, watch out!" Nancy cried, but the driver didn't seem to notice. He made a fast, reckless turn, then sped up River.

Nancy glared at it, mentally trying to fix its image in her mind. It had moved too fast for her to see the driver's face, but she was sure it was a guy—though slight of build. A slender, petite woman had been clinging to the driver, her face pressed against his back.

"Nancy, Nancy!"

At the sound of Bess's voice, Nancy turned. Bess was just outside the entrance to a store called True Blues, brandishing her camera, her face all smiles.

36

"You won't believe what just happened!" She hurried toward Nancy, breathless, her blue eyes sparkling.

Before Bess could say another word, a tall redheaded woman raced out of True Blues.

"Gotcha!" she shouted triumphantly, lunging toward Bess. Nancy watched in horror as the woman reached out and violently wrenched Bess's camera from her hands.

5

The Stalker

"Hey, that's *my* camera!" Bess shouted, struggling to grab it back. The woman pulled away from Bess, sending Bess staggering backward toward the glass window of the True Blues.

Nancy sprang into action. She reached out, clutching Bess's arm a split second before she would have hit the glass. Holding on to Bess hard, Nancy wheeled around and confronted the woman. "Give her back her camera!" Nancy insisted.

"No problem," the woman snarled. Yanking open the back of the camera, she ripped out the film and pitched it into a nearby trash can. "Here's your camera!" She tossed it toward Bess.

As Bess stood frozen, a shocked expression on her face, Nancy deftly fielded the camera.

"What right did you have to expose the—" Bess began in a shaky voice. Before she could finish her sentence, Nancy put a hand on her arm, stopping her.

Nancy had just noticed something about the woman's outfit. She was wearing slim khaki pants, with an unusual logo stitched on the pocket. Nancy remembered seeing that logo before, in the lobby of the building where her father had his office. A security and detection services company had moved into the building about a year ago. This woman was some kind of rent-a-cop. Fighting to keep the anger out of her voice, Nancy asked, "Do you work for True Blues?"

"No," the woman snapped, tossing her long red braid back from her face. "I work at Woody Acres." She seemed about to say more, then stopped herself. Meeting Nancy's level gaze, she declared, "I had every right to expose that film. Your friend had no right to take those pictures."

"The clothing store's a public place," Nancy said, defending Bess.

"The store isn't the issue here. Will Ryder is," the woman declared, her hazel eyes sparking with anger.

"Will Ryder?" Nancy's jaw dropped. She shifted her gaze to Bess, who managed a weak grin.

The guard regarded Bess grimly. Nancy noticed that though she was quite slim, she had a muscular build. "She'd better stop stalking him." With that warning the woman went to the curb, where a black and chrome Harley-Davidson was parked. After jamming a black helmet over her long red braid, she angled her bike out of the parking spot and sped away in the same direction as the first bike.

"*Stalking* Will Ryder!" Bess exclaimed in a huff.

She dusted off her light blue cropped pants. "All I was doing was taking pictures!"

"Of Will Ryder?" Nancy shook her head. "You know stars don't want their pictures taken without permission, Bess."

Bess stared at the sidewalk a second, shifting from foot to foot. Finally she looked up at Nancy, a sheepish expression on her face. "How was I supposed to know that creepo was a bodyguard?"

Nancy groaned. "That's not the point—she still had no right to treat you the way she did. Exactly what happened, Bess?"

"I'd just gotten to Sweety Pies when I saw Will Ryder and his girlfriend . . ."

"Isabel Ramos-Garcia?" Nancy had to ask. While she wasn't as big a fan of Ryder's as Bess, she did adore the pop artist's music.

"Yup!" Bess pronounced gleefully. "I'm not happy they're engaged, but imagine seeing someone like that up close and personal? Anyway, they ducked into the store—"

"And the bodyguard, did you see her?" Nancy wondered.

Bess made a face. "Guess I was too focused on Will. I waited a couple of minutes, then real casual-like walked into the store, hit one of the sale racks, and went into the dressing room—you know the one at the back. Then I peeked through the curtain and managed to snag a couple of shots. How was I supposed to know *she* was some kind of spy!"

"Bess!" Nancy exclaimed, steering Bess toward Sweety Pies. "She wasn't spying. *You* were!"

"I was just taking pictures—of people whose pictures are taken all the time," Bess protested hotly. "Anyway, that's when I first saw the guard, except I didn't realize she was a guard. I thought she was shopping like any normal person."

"So that's when she spotted you?" Nancy asked as they waited to be seated at one of the pale pink, white, and green wrought-iron tables at the sidewalk café.

"Uh—no," Bess admitted, heaving a sigh. "Isabel was rummaging through some black dresses—they were short and sexy and would look great on her. Will came up behind her and said that one of the dresses was a knockout and would be perfect for the cocktail party the night before the wedding. If she wanted it, she could have it sent back to Woody Acres. Well, I heard the word *wedding* and I gasped. That's when he and Isabel saw me and ducked out the back exit. I hurried out front hoping to catch another glimpse of them—then you saw the rest."

"Bess, you *were* wrong to take pictures without permission, but that guard was pretty rough with you. She should be reported," Nancy said.

They sat down at a corner table with a view of both the street and the river. Tourists and Saturday shoppers ambled by as the girls studied the ice-cream specials of the day and ordered sundaes.

While they waited for the waitress to bring their orders, Bess began to examine her camera. Nancy pulled a small notebook out of her pack. "I noticed the rent-a-guard logo on that woman's shirt," Nancy explained as she jotted down the name of the com-

41

pany. "But I didn't see her name. Did you?" Nancy asked.

"No," Bess said, then groaned. "I don't believe this!" She handed her camera to Nancy. "Nan, she really trashed my camera! The back won't close anymore, and this gizmo where you put in the film is broken. The camera is new, too. I can't believe that guard can get away with this."

"Maybe she can't," Nancy said. She picked up Bess's camera and examined it. It really was a mess. "That woman should pay for it," Nancy said, pulling her cell phone out of her bag.

"Who are you calling?" Bess asked as the waiter served their sundaes.

"Dad," Nancy explained. "He's got a big case going to court Monday, so he's working all weekend. He'll know if we can claim damages resulting from that guard's being too rough with you."

When her father answered, Nancy told him Bess's story.

"What did he say?" Bess asked when Nancy hung up.

"My dad was on his way to meet his client for a late lunch," Nancy reported. "But he said that the security company is open seven days, twenty-four hours a day, so he'll speak to whoever's in charge today."

"That's it?" Bess asked, sounding disappointed.

"No," Nancy said. "He also said we should meet him at the security office in an hour and a half and bring along the damaged camera."

After Nancy and Bess finished their sundaes, they picked up Nancy's Mustang and drove to Carson

Drew's office building. Nancy pointed out the lobby storefront that housed Protection and Detection. The frosted glass door was ajar. Inside the girls could see the guard from True Blues.

"What's she doing here now?" Bess exclaimed. "I hope she's not reporting *me.* Do you think your dad's been here? I'm not exactly sure I want to confront that woman until he's run interference, Nan."

"Don't worry," Nancy tried to assure her, though she had her own doubts about approaching the security company before her father intervened. Nancy had a sneaking suspicion that as mean as the guard had been, the law might be on her side.

Suddenly a man's angry voice shouted loud enough to be heard in the lobby. "Marie, you just don't get it. I called you here just now because I'm putting you on notice. Your job is watching Will Ryder's back, not causing major P.R. problems for this company. A big-wig lawyer registered a complaint about you today. If you don't shape up, I'm going to dock your pay . . . or give you the boot."

"Marie was only trying to do her job," another male voice argued.

"Cool it, Bruce. The last thing I need is for *you* to stand up for me!"

Nancy beckoned Bess to follow as she quietly moved closer to the door. Fortunately, since it was Saturday, the usually busy lobby was deserted: even the newsstand was closed. No one would notice them eavesdropping. Nancy pretended to study the building directory, keeping her ears trained on the argument in the security company offices.

43

"Hey, I'm just trying to be helpful here," the voice belonging to the guy called Bruce protested.

"Look, Mr. Korinthenos," Marie went on, addressing the other man, "I'm just trying to do my job. I can't help it if Will and Isabel are making things tough for me. Cruising around town on a motorcycle is no way to keep a low profile. He should be in a car or, better yet, a limo. If Will's so worried about paparazzi, he should travel so people can't spot him so easily."

"A limo is like a neon sign that says, 'Star Inside!' " Mr. Korinthenos went on. "This way Will and Isabel can blend in with the crowd. A couple on a motorcycle with the visors of their helmets down is far less eye-catching than some limo."

"Whatever!" Marie declared brusquely. "Whatever problems crop up, I'm good at my job. And I *know* exactly what my job is: Keeping cameras away from Will Ryder this weekend is my top priority." She paused, then added sarcastically, "Maybe it's Bruce here who'd better shape up. Like, where was he last night when someone tried to break into Woody Acres? That happened on your watch, Bruce, not mine!"

"Break in!" Nancy whistled softly. "Bess, maybe that's what the prowler was doing last night—trying to keep tabs on Will Ryder."

"And to photograph his wedding!" Bess added.

Nancy nodded. "That would mean major-league bucks for some tabloid photographer." More than enough motive for attempting to trespass onto a heavily secured estate.

"Marie," Mr. Korinthenos spoke up testily. "You can protest all you want, but you're the one who dropped the ball here. Lucky for you, it was just some silly fan with a point-and-shoot camera who breached your security in that shop. Otherwise, we'd be in deep trouble with Ryder's people. As it stands now, I have to pay for a camera that you did not have to break to expose the film. Your pay will be docked for the price of the camera, Ms. Russo."

Nancy and Bess backed into the center of the lobby just as Marie stomped out the door. She crossed the marble floor with her head down, but as she reached the revolving door she looked up—right at Bess.

"You again—here?" Marie shook her head in disbelief. "Haven't you caused enough trouble today?" Marie glared at Bess, then continued toward the door. Just before she reached it, she turned. "You'd better watch your step, or you'll be sorry you ever *heard* of Will Ryder!"

6

Bess Makes a Promise

"Did you hear that?" Bess gasped, leaning back against the lobby kiosk. "That woman actually threatened me!"

"Look, Bess," Nancy said, hastening to calm her friend, "she's just freaked because her boss is going to dock her pay. She's venting, that's all."

"Yeah—I guess. . . . I just hope I don't keep running into her." Bess bit her lower lip. "Hey, Nan, maybe I should just forget about the camera—it wasn't *that* expensive and—"

"No way," Nancy stated firmly, steering Bess toward the Protection and Detection office. "You heard that Mr. Korinthenos. They're going to pay for a new one. You are not backing down now."

"I'm not?" Bess sounded dubious, but she followed Nancy into the agency office. As the girls opened the frosted glass door, the two men inside stopped talking and looked up. Nancy quickly took in her surroundings. Like all the lobby offices in the building, this one was small, with just enough room for a large wooden desk, an area for a copy machine, fax, printer, and a couple of chairs. The door to the tiny back room was open, revealing a bank of file cabinets.

The man seated at the desk regarded Nancy with a frank open gaze. Nancy judged him to be in his early fifties, with fading blond hair and a receding hairline. His tie was loosened, and his suit jacket was draped on the back of his chair. The office was uncomfortably warm and stuffy.

The other man was younger, in his early twenties. He wore a company logo shirt and tan trousers. He smiled broadly first at Nancy, then Bess. He had brown eyes, medium brown hair cropped close, and a slender but muscular build. "Hey!" he said after a second. "Can we help you?"

Before Nancy could answer, the man behind the desk stood up. "I have a pretty good idea who you are," he said, addressing Nancy. "Carson Drew's daughter." Reaching across the desk he pumped Nancy's hand. "Your father spoke to me earlier. And I imagine you are the young woman who has a claim about a camera," the man said pleasantly, turning toward Bess. "I never did get your name from Mr. Drew."

Bess swallowed nervously, then answered. "Bess. Bess Marvin."

"I'm Demo Korinthenos, president of Protection and Detection. This," he added, pointing to the younger man, "is Bruce Lankowski, one of my top security guards."

Bruce straightened up, grinned at the girls, and gave a little salute.

Mr. Korinthenos cleared his throat. "I am very sorry, Ms. Marvin, for the incident this afternoon. Marie Russo did step over the line."

"So you'll pay for a new one?" Bess asked, relieved.

"Or we'll have it fixed. Did you bring it along?"

Bess dug in her pale straw carryall and handed over the camera. Bruce watched closely as Mr. Korinthenos examined it.

"Where's the film?" Bruce asked, his eyes were bright, curious, eager. Nancy instantly pegged him as a flirt—a rather cute flirt.

That Bess had drawn the same conclusion was obvious. She lowered her long, thick lashes and blushed a little before answering.

"The guard tossed it into the garbage," Bess added with a plaintive note in her voice.

"I know you're disappointed, Ms. Marvin, but we couldn't allow you to walk away with the film intact. But as I said, Marie overstepped her bounds, and she shouldn't have broken your camera, and I do apologize. He handed Bess back her camera. "I can see this is beyond fixing. We'll pay for a new one—and throw in a roll of film as a favor to your father," Mr. Korinthenos told Nancy. "I hope you won't try to take any more snapshots of Mr. Ryder," he admonished Bess.

"I won't," Bess vowed.

"Besides," Bruce spoke up, "it's not safe hanging around the estate. We've had prowlers there lately—"

"Paparazzi?" Nancy supplied, remembering what

48

she and Bess had just overheard through the open door of the office.

Bruce raised his eyebrows. "You're quick!"

"Thanks," Nancy said, surprised at the compliment. Turning to Mr. Korinthenos, she added, "And thank you, too. Is there anything else we need to do about the camera?"

"Oh, yes. I'll need the receipt—if you still have it," the company owner told Bess.

"Sure. I bought the camera just a couple of weeks ago. I'll get the receipt now and bring it right back."

"Then I'll see you later," Mr. Korinthenos said, walking them to the office door.

"I'd better hit the road now, too," Bruce said, grabbing a set of keys off a hook by the water cooler. He headed into the lobby with Nancy and Bess.

Bruce fell into step with them as Bess headed for the exit. "Where are you guys going now?"

"I'm walking home," Bess informed him. She hung back a little, and Nancy could tell Bess was hoping Bruce would offer her a ride.

"And I'm going upstairs to see if my father's back from lunch," Nancy added.

Bruce nodded, then asked Nancy, "I couldn't help but notice your Star Wares bag. Are you into astronomy?"

Nancy lifted her shoulders. "Not yet. But I could easily get hooked on it. I'm going back to check out Dr. Stars tonight. He's giving a lecture in the park. You should drop by."

Bruce mugged a face. "Can't. Duty calls. I'm scheduled to work Woody Acres."

"Lucky you," Bess mumbled.

Bruce playfully wagged a finger under Bess's nose. "Now, now. You promised . . ."

"Not to take pictures." Bess returned his smile. "But I can still *look* at Will Ryder if I happen to run into him."

"Well, don't just *happen* to turn up at Woody Acres— you wouldn't want to get Marie all steamed up again," Bruce warned with a hearty laugh. "Hey, if you're good, and stay away, maybe I'll snare the guy's autograph and pass it on to you when we replace your camera."

"Really!" Bess clasped her hands in front of her and broke into a wide smile.

"If I can—but no promises—I'm just a guard on the estate." With that Bruce waved goodbye and hurried outside.

Before Bess left, she asked Nancy, "Are you really going back to the park tonight?"

"Wouldn't miss it. I really want to see what Dr. Stars is all about. George is coming. You should, too."

"You couldn't pay me a million bucks to go back there."

"Even though Dr. Stars isn't so bad to look at?" Nancy teased.

Bess giggled. "I'd rather skip the outdoors stuff tonight, maybe check out a club. You don't mind?"

"No." Nancy smiled warmly. "Whatever, have a good time . . . and stay away from Will Ryder!"

Laughing, Bess pushed through the revolving door. Nancy walked to the bank of elevators and pressed the Up button, happy that the problem with Bess's camera seemed to be solved. So was the mystery of last night's prowler. The shadow she saw darting through the woods was probably nothing more sinister than a fan or reporter trying to scope out Will Ryder's hideaway.

Still, the missing focusing knob on Dr. Stars's telescope niggled at the back of Nancy's mind. She'd get to the park early enough to search the grass around the embankment, to see what she could find.

The elevator *binged.* The door whooshed open, and Nancy's father stepped out.

"Dad!" She started to greet him when the squeal of tires, followed by a bloodcurdling scream, echoed throughout the lobby.

7

A Sudden Blaze of Light

Nancy's smile froze on her face. "That sounded like Bess screaming!" she cried in horror. Nancy pelted across the lobby and rushed outside. There was no sign of a traffic accident.

But a small crowd was gathered halfway down the block. Nancy caught a glimpse of a familiar blond head. It *was* Bess. She was leaning against a brick wall, the color drained from her face, her bag on the ground, its contents scattered. Still, she was standing up and didn't look hurt.

Nancy bolted down the street to Bess's side. "Are you all right?" she gasped, grabbing Bess's hand, as Mr. Drew sprinted up.

At Nancy's touch Bess burst into tears.

"Bess, are you all right?" Carson Drew asked.

Bess managed a nod.

"Only because she's got good reflexes," an older

woman added. "That motorcycle took that corner like a maniac!"

Shading her eyes from the sun, Nancy looked at the woman. "Did you get the plate number? What kind of bike was it?"

The woman shrugged as Bess's sobs subsided. "Sorry. They all look alike to me. Though this was definitely black," she added. "And big."

"Right," a girl in a bright yellow T-shirt spoke up. "It was a Harley." She was gathering Bess's stuff off the sidewalk. She put everything back in the bag and handed it to Nancy.

Bess wiped the tears off her face and clutched Nancy's arm. "Marie Russo drives a Harley," she said, her voice low and shaky. "It was her. She's out to hurt me!"

"I don't know, Bess," Nancy said doubtfully. "Lots of people drive Harleys. Did you see her face?"

Before Nancy could ask if Bess had noticed Marie's red braid, Carson Drew asked Bess directly."What exactly happened, Bess?" He steadied Bess as she straightened up. "You're sure you're not hurt?"

"I'm okay, Mr. Drew. Really." Bess managed a weak smile. "Just got the wind knocked out of me."

As the crowd dispersed, Mr. Drew said quietly to Bess. "Now, who is the 'she' who's out to hurt you?"

"I'm sure I know who it was," Bess added as they started walking toward Nancy's car.

"You recognized the driver?" Mr. Drew asked.

Bess closed her eyes and breathed out slowly. "No. It happened so fast. But it had to be that security guard who broke my camera."

"Bess, you can't be sure of that," Nancy protested.

"What makes you think it's her, Bess?" Mr. Drew asked. "That's a pretty serious accusation."

"I know. But Nancy—you heard her. She threatened me right outside the Protection and Detection office."

"She *warned* you, Bess—to stay away from Will Ryder," Nancy reminded her. "Why would she try to run you over?"

"Maybe she's mad because her pay's going to be docked," Bess pointed out.

"She was way out of line," Nancy agreed, though still doubtful.

Her father thought for a moment, then asked, "Is there anything I can do?"

"No, Dad. Not yet. Let me look into this."

Carson arched his eyebrows, and his lips twitched into a small smile. "Now, how did I know you were going to say that? But be careful, Nancy. If Bess *is* right, you could be dealing with someone very dangerous here."

"True." Nancy smiled ruefully. "But at the moment I'm going to give Bess a ride home so she can pick up her receipt."

Bess gave a small shudder. "I'm not really looking forward to walking back in there again."

"You don't have to," Mr. Drew suggested. "You can fax the receipt from the copy shop near your house, Bess."

Relief washed over Bess's features. "Great idea. Thanks."

Mr. Drew said, "See you later for dinner?"

"For dinner, yes," Nancy answered. "But George

54

and I are heading to the state park later for Dr. Stars's sky tour."

"Maybe it'll actually happen this time," Bess remarked.

"Now, this is more like it!" George said that evening as Nancy scrounged for a parking space in the state park's lot. "Looks like half of River Heights turned out."

Nancy grinned. "And the real star party is tomorrow."

George looked amused. "So what's the difference between a star watch and a star party?"

"I'm not sure," Nancy admitted. "But I don't think Dr. Stars will be lecturing at the star party. And according to Richard—that guy in Star Wares—there'll be a ton of telescopes at the party. Everyone who has one brings it along. But I bet *all* of the local astronomy crowd is here tonight."

As Nancy slowly circled the lot, she was surprised by the diversity of the would-be stargazers. She had expected slightly geeky, science types, but they were mixed with families, a number of senior citizens, and a group that looked like college students.

Nancy finally sandwiched her Mustang between two SUVs. She reached into the glove compartment, pocketed her flashlight, then checked to see that the penlight on her key chain was working.

Nancy glanced at her watch. It was a little before nine. Twilight was already deep, with just the ruddy remains of sunset staining the western horizon. Nancy had hoped to arrive while there was still enough light to search for the focusing knob. By the time dessert was finished, though, she'd left a good half hour later than she'd intended.

As on the night before, the area lights were turned off. "Remember I told you I picked up a book at Star Wares today?" she asked George. "Well, it explained why the street lamps are out."

"Not budget cuts?" George laughed. "Or is there a new project to protect the night-owl population in the park?"

"No!" Nancy said, pretending to be offended. "Astronomers are really serious about safeguarding their night vision. Did you know some of them won't go anywhere during the day without really dark sunglasses? Apparently, they shun bright light the way cats avoid water."

George nodded. "That makes sense. I sort of figured that the lights were out the other night because they'd interfere with stargazing."

"Maybe Dr. Stars can tell us more about that," Nancy suggested as they joined the audience near the van. Four or five telescopes were set up in the lot, all oriented in a north-to-northeast direction. A few people were already lined up to look through the largest scope.

As Nancy had promised Bess the previous evening, the crowd was weighted heavily in the direction of young, college-age guys.

"Bess is going to kill herself for not coming," George whispered to Nancy. "This is primo flirt territory!"

Nancy wasn't quite sure. "It could be—if you could get their eyes off the sky for a minute."

As they settled in on top of a picnic table, Bob Steller caught their eye and smiled. "Two diehards," he said, strolling up. "Nancy Drew and George, right?" he asked.

Nancy nodded and asked. "Did you ever find that knob for the telescope?"

"No, I didn't. But I took one off a camera, and the knob fits well enough to do the trick."

"They probably have knobs downtown at Star Wares—I was there today checking out the telescopes," Nancy told him.

"You were?"

"So was Derek Randall," George added.

"Is he here tonight?" Dr. Stars scanned the crowd.

"Not that I see," Nancy said, remembering that the two rival astronomers had yet to meet in person.

"Good!" he said. "I don't need that aggravation. But it's time to get started. Thanks for turning up again after last night," he repeated. He clapped his hands and waited for the crowd to quiet down.

"I'm glad to see such a big turnout," Dr. Stars twanged. His voice carried surprisingly well. Except for the huskiness, it was a good stage voice, Nancy mused as he continued, "You guys really lucked out. The weather is perfect for stargazing. It's the dark of the moon and prime time for one of the major events of the stargazing year: the Perseid meteor shower. Tonight let's talk about Perseids and meteors in general—but briefly, so we can get to the business of stargazing."

Dr. Stars pulled a stack of index cards from his vest pocket, ran his penlight over them, then asked, "Who here knows about this Perseid meteor shower?"

A scattering of hands shot up. Dr. Stars pointed to a boy, who said, "It happens the same time every year—all the meteor showers do—so you can plan to come out and watch them."

"Why is that?" Dr. Stars asked. "Why do they happen at the same time? Why the name *the Perseids*?" He pointed to another upraised hand.

This time an older girl answered. "Because it comes from the constellation named Perseus," she said confidently.

"Good!" Dr. Stars congratulated her.

Several hands shot up, and a murmur ran through the crowd. Dr. Stars called on a young man in his twenties. "That's dead wrong! It's called the Perseids because it *appears* to come from Perseus. But of course, that's nonsense." The man added smugly, "As you well know!"

Dr. Stars drew a quick intake of breath. "Caught me, did you? I do like to bait the trap." He cast an apologetic look at the girl, then nodded at the young man. "Want to shed some light on the subject?"

The guy shrugged. "Sure. Everyone knows that the meteors we see are in *this* solar system. The constellation Perseus is made up of stars that are light-years away from our sun.

"Meteors are pieces of rock that orbit the Sun, just as the Earth and other planets do, but in a different sort of orbit," the young man went on. "And when the orbits of a particular bunch of meteors intersect with ours—like the Perseids in August—small particles get caught in our atmosphere, and we see shooting stars."

Dr. Stars picked up the narrative. "Which, of course, are just particles of dust, for the most part, meteorites that travel through the atmosphere—though sometimes they are really large and fall to

Earth." He stopped and gestured toward the western horizon. All traces of the sunset were gone, and the sky was bright with stars. "But enough talk. Let's get to these telescopes. I oriented them for a good view of the major constellations."

As people scrambled to their feet to line up behind various scopes, Dr. Stars handed out lists of stars and constellations to look for in the sky.

Using Nancy's penlight, she and George studied their list. "Nan, I read somewhere that there's a double star system in the handle of the Big Dipper," George said. "Dr. Stars has it here on his list. He says you can see it through a pair of good-quality binoculars. There's also a ton of double stars in a constellation called Lyra. Let's scope it out!"

Nancy agreed, nodding toward the giant binoculars. "If regular binoculars work, imagine how good those are."

"Besides, the line for the binoculars is the shortest—like just one person," George pointed out. The binoculars were mounted on a sturdy tripod, at the farthest end of the semicircle of telescopes. Unlike the telescopes, the binoculars were oriented north to slightly northwest, the same direction as the telescope Derek had moved the night before.

As George and Nancy approached the binoculars, the person looking through them straightened up.

Nancy grabbed George's elbow. "I know her," she whispered. The young woman's hair was no longer in a braid: it fell in a thick mane of curls halfway down her back. In the dark its color was indecipherable, but Nancy recognized the woman. "That's Marie Russo!"

George gasped. "The bodyguard who attacked Bess?"

"What's she doing here?" Nancy wondered. Then she frowned as Marie looked around furtively, and changed the viewing angle, tilting the binoculars toward the valley.

"More like what's she doing period?" George murmured. "I think we should get Dr. Stars." But even before George had finished her sentence, Marie had readjusted the binoculars to approximate their original viewing angle. Checking back over her shoulder, she proceeded toward Dr. Stars's van. Though it was now totally dark, Nancy could see Marie creep up to the vehicle. The young woman cast another stealthy glance behind her, then aimed a small flashlight through the back window. The curtains across the window were open now.

"What's she up to?" George murmured.

"No good, that's for sure!" Nancy whispered. The girls moved closer to the van. Whatever had brought the bodyguard here, Nancy would bet a million dollars it had nothing to do with stargazing.

"Hey, Nancy Drew, I made it after all!" a voice called out.

Nancy did an about-face. "Richard!" she said, recognizing the clerk from Star Wares. He was standing next to a Volkswagen Bug, its trunk open. A Jeep was pulled up next to him, its engine running.

"Wait up," he called to her, then said something to the driver of the Jeep before it pulled away. As Richard closed the trunk of the VW and approached, Nancy silently cursed his timing. She didn't want to lose track of Marie. She glanced toward the van, but her line of sight was blocked. "You didn't have to work, after all?" she asked Richard.

"I did. But we closed half an hour ago. So I'm here. Too late for the lecture. Though I hear the doctor's proving to be a bit of a dud."

"What do you mean?" George asked, curious.

Richard jerked his head back toward the Jeep, its receding taillights still visible as it turned onto the park drive. "Those guys from the astronomy club are convinced Stars is all hype. I heard he flubbed some really basic question about where the Perseid meteor shower originated."

Nancy shrugged. "He said he was just testing the audience."

"Maybe, but then one of my pals overheard him talking pure nonsense to some poor kid. He got the terms for meteor, meteoroid, and meteorite mixed up—a meteorite's what hits the ground and he said they're what sail through space."

George shrugged. "I think he's just a bit flaky."

"It sounds more like major memory lapses."

Nancy frowned. "Maybe. I'd like to hear more, Richard. But can it wait a few minutes? I was checking out something when you walked up."

"Marie!" George groaned. "I forgot all about her."

Nancy turned quickly toward the van. The small crowd had broken up. No one was around the back of Dr. Stars's vehicle.

Marie had vanished. Nancy shook her head in disgust. "We lost her, George," she murmured, then out of the corner of her eye she glimpsed a shadowy figure skirting the edge of the crowd. Most heads were turned up toward the sky. But this person's head was low, keeping his or her face hidden.

Nancy couldn't confirm that it was Marie, but every instinct told her it had to be. Instantly Nancy went in pursuit, threading her way through the crowd.

"Hey, watch out!" some man cried, grabbing Nancy's arm, just in time to keep her from tripping over a child asleep in a stroller.

"Sorry!" Nancy apologized. By the time she looked back toward the picnic area, the figure was hitting the path to the woods.

This is impossible! Nancy grumbled inwardly.

All at once every streetlight in the area flashed on.

The figure's head jerked up, turned, and peered back for a second.

Nancy shielded her eyes from the sudden glare. "Marie!" she cried, recognizing the girl instantly.

The guard regarded Nancy, an expression of pure panic on her face.

8

A Creak in the Night

The lights blazed up. The crowd groaned, dismayed.

"What just happened?" George looked around. The stargazers' good mood had suddenly shifted. Everyone was squinting, rubbing their eyes against the glare, and they all appeared to be annoyed and frustrated.

"What happened is someone blew it big time," Richard remarked, clearly exasperated. "Now everyone's night vision will be ruined for hours." He shrugged and said, "People might as well go home—unless they had planned on an all-nighter and the park decides to turn off the wattage."

In the glare, Nancy was able to read the fear and panic on Marie's face. The woman was staring directly at someone to Nancy's right. Nancy followed her gaze and was startled to see Bruce—the other guard from Protection and Detection—looking darkly in Marie's direction. Was it Nancy's imagination or had Marie quickly looked away?

When Nancy turned back to see where Marie was going, she had already vanished. Why do I have the impression that Marie was avoiding Bruce? Nancy wondered. She threaded her way through the people streaming back to their cars. "Hey, Bruce," Nancy called out to him.

At the sight of her Bruce changed his scowl to a pleasant smile. "Hey, Nancy!" He paused. "Bet you wondered if I'm goofing off—"

"You *did* say you'd be working at the estate," Nancy reminded him.

"I *am*. Actually that's why I'm here. But let Dr. Stars explain what's happening."

"Yo! People!" Dr. Stars was standing on a picnic table, improvising a megaphone with his hands. Heads turned. People stopped in their tracks.

"Sorry about the lights on—but I just heard from the park rangers that there's been a prowler in the vicinity," Dr. Stars explained.

A murmur went up from the crowd.

The astronomer's face crinkled into a frown. He threw up his hands. "Don't panic. I'm sure the authorities have the situation under control. But we've got to shut ourselves down early tonight. Sorry about that—but remember the River Heights Astronomy Club is holding a Perseids star party here tomorrow, and I'll be around to answer any more questions."

"Boy, this man is having no luck with this stop on his Star Van tour! He's going to think River Heights is jinxed!" Richard mumbled, reaching in his pocket for his car keys. "Guess I'll hit the road. See you tomorrow night, Nancy?"

"Right. Complete with camera," she told him, then started for her car with George.

As soon as they were out of earshot, George said to Nancy, "Did you hear what Richard said—about Dr. Stars being jinxed here?"

"I did," Nancy admitted. "And I wonder. There's no better way to kill a star party than to flood the observing area with bright light."

"Maybe that prowler has nothing to do with Woody Acres, Nancy. Maybe it's someone out to throw a wrench in the works for Dr. Stars."

"My very thought." Nancy nodded. "And we're both thinking that that someone might be Derek Randall."

"But he wasn't here tonight."

"But why not, George? He was supposed to check this scene out. He wanted to meet his 'rival.' Then this afternoon he said he couldn't make it. But it seems very convenient he wasn't around when things went wrong," Nancy pointed out. She rubbed her temples. "To tell you the truth this all feels like one big muddle to me. On the one hand, we know Dr. Stars has an enemy in Derek Randall. And then on the other hand—completely unconnected—we see Marie snooping around Dr. Stars's van. But why?"

George shrugged. "Beats me, Nan. Unless she was also looking for this prowler."

Nancy shook her head vehemently. "No. I don't think she's on duty tonight. And why did she look so freaked to see Bruce?"

Calling Dr. Stars. Have the e-mail goblins captured you—or intercepted your latest sendings? I haven't heard from you since Thursday night. Part of our deal was for me to swelter in this Amazonian jungle-land, gathering botanical samples from treetops, while you do your summer Star Van thing and tour the lovely temperate States. I've kept my end of the bargain: One e-mail a day keeps loneliness away. But my last two sendings were never even called up. What kind of stars are you watching, babe? Hopefully not the Hollywood kind. I'm worried enough to post this in a public place so that you'll be so embarrassed you'll rush to e-mail me just to shut me up. It's Saturday going on Sunday here. Where in the Universe are you? Don't tell me you finally fell into a black hole!!!

Nancy read the note posted on the message board of Dr. Stars's Web site. It was from Dr. Stars's wife, Teresa. Nancy had already happened on Teresa Steller's Eco-Jungle page when she did a search for Dr. Stars. The female Dr. Steller turned out to be an eco-botanist currently working in the Amazon. The light, humorous tone of her note didn't fool Nancy. The woman was clearly worried about her husband.

Why wasn't Dr. Stars responding to his wife's messages? One more oddly unsettling fact surrounding Dr. Stars's visit to the area.

Earlier, unable to shake off a vague feeling of foreboding, Nancy had come home from that night's abbreviated star watch and had headed for the study to investigate Dr. Stars on the computer. She was relieved to find that both Hannah and her dad had already turned in for the night. Except for the foyer light, and her dad's green shaded desk lamp, the house was dark and quiet, providing the perfect setting for Nancy to try to sort out her thoughts. So far her computer research had proved interesting but not fruitful.

On the one hand she was put off by Dr. Stars's Web site—mainly because of that silly cartoon logo. Nancy couldn't fathom why such a handsome man would choose to picture himself as an older, nerdy guy. On the other hand the site was marvelously designed, with a generous sprinkling of Dr. Stars's drawings, digital photos of all sorts of astronomical phenomena, plus wonderful hyperlinks to other astronomical sites. Nancy found herself able to surf to NASA's site, to amazing star charts, and even to Web sites for Mt. Palomar Observatory in California, and Mauna Loa in Hawaii.

The whole thing was more in sync with the Dr. Stars revealed by her glimpse into his journal, not by the somewhat absentminded guy at the star watch tonight. What did Richard call his mistakes—major memory lapses? Well, what did she expect from a guy who forgot to leave a note explaining his whereabouts his first night at the state park.

Nancy decided he had had a professional design the site.

"Now is this a weird coincidence or what?" Nancy murmured as she reread Teresa Steller's posting.

Bob Steller's wife hadn't heard from him in two days, not since Thursday night. Nancy drummed her fingers against the desk, then she flipped back a page in her notebook to Friday night. Sure enough. The entries in Dr. Stars's diary had also stopped Friday.

Friday, yesterday, the night she had first encountered Derek Randall. Nancy leaned back in the roomy leather-covered desk chair and tapped her pen against her chin. Come to think of it, what exactly did she know about this Randall guy, anyway? Only what he'd told her. Just that he taught at Grimsley College near L.A., and of course, *his* version of his rivalry with Dr. Stars.

Nancy rolled her chair closer to the desk and punched in Derek Randall's name.

The search engine turned up about three dozen Derek Randall hits, but only one for an astronomer. Unlike Dr. Stars's flashy graphic and animation-filled page, Derek's was conservative, quiet, boring, and very academic. Exactly, Nancy reflected, like the man.

She quickly scanned his personal information, but nothing struck her as surprising. Web sites linked to his were pretty much the same batch as those on Dr. Stars's page, except for one—Hot Stars: Hot Topics.

Nancy decided to try it. She found herself at the site of a forum on controversial astronomical issues. There were postings that ranged from irate comments about why waste good money on SETI—the group that conducted organized radio astronomy searches for extraterrestrial life in the universe, when humans on Earth were starving—to ongoing arguments over manned versus unmanned space exploration.

She checked the most recent entries on the screen. One was posted earlier that week from an amateur astronomer somewhere in Iowa. Dr. Stars's Star Van had been in town. The posting accused Dr. Stars of being out for glory and playing dirty with Derek Randall—who "rumor has it, is fit to kill over the academic guerrilla warfare being waged by the popular Dr. Stars."

Nancy's blood froze as she read the posting. A very clear picture of Derek Randall lurking around the Star Van Friday night formed in Nancy's mind. He had almost knocked her over a cliff—with the excuse that he was trying to keep *her* from knocking over Dr. Stars's telescope.

He had begged off attending the star watch this evening, even though he'd seemed greatly interested in "putting a face to the name" and meeting his arch rival only twenty-four hours before. Then Dr. Stars's whole lecture and demonstration was botched by another "prowler" incident.

Could Derek be behind it all? He had the motive and the know-how.

The thought had barely taken hold when Nancy heard a strange sound outside the slightly open study window. She turned to look, but the curtain was drawn. It lifted gently in the breeze. Nancy shrugged and refocused on the computer monitor. Something creaked behind her.

Nancy's heart began to pound. Was she imagining things or were unseen hands pushing the window open wider?

9

Star Sightings

Nancy's heart leaped into her throat. Someone was definitely raising the sash of the partially open window. Though her pulse was racing, she pretended not to have heard the sound. She continued to focus on the computer screen. Unfortunately the monitor was angled so she couldn't catch the reflection of the intruder. Without averting her gaze, Nancy slid her hand off the mouse and across the desktop until her fingers closed on a heavy glass paperweight. Trying to steady her breathing, she began to visualize exactly how she'd attack the interloper.

The window suddenly squeaked loudly. Nancy leaped up and whirled around, the paperweight raised above her head.

"Bess!" she gasped as Bess poked her head through the open window.

"Sorry," Bess apologized, trying to extricate herself

from the curtains. "It's late and I didn't want to ring the doorbell. I noticed the light on in the study, and when I looked in the window, I saw you."

"Come around front," Nancy told her, putting down the paperweight and going to open the door.

A moment later Bess was in the study. She flipped her hair back and flopped down on the couch. She seemed totally recovered from her bad experiences earlier in the day. Her cheeks were a healthy pink. Her blue eyes were bright with excitement. "Something so excellent has happened, I just had to come to get you."

"Now? It's nearly midnight, Bess." Nancy blew out her breath. "Really, you half scared me out of my skin." She settled down in a chair across from Bess and grinned. "So what could possibly be happening at this hour that couldn't wait until morning."

"The midnight sci-fi show at the Downtown Multiplex."

Nancy started to laugh. "This is a bit of a detour."

Bess ignored Nancy's comment. Sitting forward on the couch, she enthused, "But wait until you hear the real scoop. I was home trying to forget all about that horror, Marie, when Lindsay Schmidt phoned."

"Lindsay from high school?" Nancy remarked. "How's she doing? What's she up to?"

"She's great—I think. I mean we didn't talk about what we were up to, except that she's working at the multiplex this summer, taking tickets. You won't believe who's there tonight—disguised, of course—"

Nancy winced. "Let me guess—Will Ryder! Now, Bess—" Nancy began to warn.

"You don't need to 'now, Bess' me, Nan. The theater's a public place, and he's there *now*. Going to the same movie he's at is *not stalking* him. And you know I don't even own a *working* camera at the moment, thanks to you-know-who!"

Nancy made a calming gesture with her hands. "Okay. I've got the picture. Except why are you *here* then and not at the theater?"

"You. I want you to come with me. George wasn't in the mood and I don't want to go alone," Bess confessed. "It wouldn't be much fun. Plus if I do miss him, I'd have to sit through a possibly terrifying classic sci-fi flick all by myself!"

Nancy glanced back at her computer. She was more in the mood to finish checking out the Dr. Stars–Derek Randall connection. Reading the comment about Derek Randall being fit to kill Dr. Stars had almost convinced Nancy that Dr. Stars's visit to River Heights was being sabotaged. "I'm not in the mood for the midnight movie scene." River Heights's midnight movie crowd was boisterous and notorious for chanting every line of dialogue with the actors in the film.

"Why not?" Bess asked in a reasonable tone. "Seems to me you aren't in bed yet. You don't look remotely sleepy. Don't tell me you prefer surfing the Web to my fun company."

Nancy giggled. "You've got a point. I'm too hyped up to sleep." She hesitated only a minute. Staying home wouldn't solve anything. A sci-fi thriller might be just the thing to distract her. "Oh, why not? I'm game, Bess. Let me get my sweater and put my shoes back on, and we'll drive downtown. If we leave in a minute or two, we'll even be on time."

Ten minutes later they arrived at the Downtown Multiplex. The six-theater complex occupied a former herb and spice warehouse on the fringe of the River Front district. The neighborhood still had seedy edges, but the area around the theater and the parking lot across the street were well lit.

Ignoring the lure of popcorn in the lobby, Bess marched Nancy right into Theater 3. "Let's sit in back, Nan, on the aisle," Bess whispered as the house lights dimmed. "I'll have a better view of the audience!"

"Go for it!" Nancy whispered back. Bess promptly steered her into the last row of the center aisle. Except for the last three rows, the theater was fairly packed.

The trailer for the first preview began, and Nancy settled comfortably in her seat. Bess was right, a movie was just what Nancy needed to relax. She'd have a better take on what Derek was up to in the morning.

Bess clutched Nancy's arm and pointed. "It's them. Over there! That's Will Ryder," she cried in a low whisper.

Nancy straightened up. She spied a slight young man getting out of the aisle seat a couple of rows in front of them. He bent down to speak to his date, a petite dark-haired woman. Light from the movie screen bathed her face, and Nancy saw clearly that it was Isabel Ramos-Garcia. She was even more beautiful in person than on video or screen.

"He's getting popcorn, Nancy!" Bess announced, her eyes glued to Will Ryder.

"Stop staring, Bess. He'll notice you."

"That's the point." Bess grinned.

"Not!" Nancy remonstrated. "If he sees you watching him, he's going to leave."

Bess obediently turned and looked straight ahead, while Will Ryder hurried up the darkened aisle. Nancy could feel Bess's whole body tense up as the guy passed. As he opened the door to the lobby, a slice of light lit up the back row across from Nancy. She noticed a man sitting by himself in the last row of the side aisle. The lobby door closed. The theater went dark again, before Nancy could make out his face.

"Come on. *We're* getting popcorn," Bess informed her, then bolted out to the concession stand.

As Nancy got out of her seat, the man across the aisle jumped up and raced out after Bess.

For a moment Nancy just stared after him. Bess running after Will Ryder made sense. Nancy herself was thrilled at the prospect of seeing the star in real life.

But a grown man? Why would *he* be chasing a teen heartthrob? Unless—Nancy barely stifled an exclamation. Was he a paparazzo? Maybe even the same "prowler" that had been skulking around Woody Acres Estate the past couple of nights?

Curiosity propelled Nancy after him. Nancy quickly took in the lobby: a bank of Plexiglas candy dispensers filled with colorful sweets lined one wall. An escalator leading to Theaters 4, 5, and 6 was off to Nancy's left. And she was face-to-face with a larger-than-life freestanding cardboard cutout of a cartoon superhero. But neither Bess nor the man was anywhere in sight.

Will Ryder was. Though he was slighter than he appeared on screen, Nancy had to admit he was even hotter looking in person. His dark curly hair poked out rakishly from beneath a Cubs baseball cap, worn with the visor toward the back. His eyes were big and a startling shade of blue. The vendor at the concession stand looked like she was about to melt into the butter as she handed him a tub of popcorn and some change. He turned to head back into the theater. Nancy quickly averted her gaze and spotted a movement behind the cardboard cartoon character.

A man poked his head out, an ultra-small point-and-shoot camera in one hand.

"Dr. Steller!" Nancy exclaimed, amazed.

"Nancy?" His face registered pure dismay. Quickly he stuffed the mini-camera into his vest pocket. His shocked expression was abruptly replaced by his familiar vague and friendly smile.

"What are you doing here?" they asked in unison.

With a bemused grin, Dr. Steller shrugged. "Those lights coming on in the parking lot killed my stargazing for the night. And I've always been a sci-fi fan."

Nancy eyed Dr. Steller's vest. She *had* seen a camera. For the moment, though, she'd play dumb. "Funny, I was just checking out your Web page about an hour ago. I read that it was reruns of that old TV series, *Star Hunters,* that first inspired you to study astronomy."

"Right—when I was a boy," he said, a note of relief in his voice.

Nancy was about to bring up the subject of the camera, when Bess stomped up, furious.

"Your camera scared him away!" she cried.

"Uh—what camera?" Dr. Stars acted befuddled.

Bess ignored the question and pointed her finger

toward the exit. With his sunglasses down, and the visor of his cap pulled low over his face, Will was scurrying toward the door, Isabel beside him.

"Look who else is here!" Bess remarked as Bruce the bodyguard stepped into the theater lobby. He said something to Will Ryder, then spotted Nancy, Bess, and Dr. Stars and scowled. Still shaking his head, he followed the two celebrities out onto the street.

"You're lucky Bruce didn't confiscate your camera," Nancy said, turning back to Dr. Steller.

The astronomer continued to play dumb. "Confiscate what?"

"This!" With a neat swift movement Nancy plucked the camera out of Dr. Stars's pocket.

For a second Nancy thought she detected a flicker of anger in the man's eyes. But he sagged back against the wall and flashed her a boyish, goofy grin. "Busted!" he conceded. "It must seem pretty out there for a guy like me to be trying to take a snapshot of a heartthrob like this Ryder guy. But I've got a kid sister back home who worships the ground the guy walks on."

"Yeah." Bess frowned. "But how'd you know he'd be here? It wasn't exactly on the eleven o'clock news."

"I didn't," Dr. Stars protested, then caught Nancy's eye. He shrugged again. "Like you said. I'm into sci-fi flicks."

"And you just happened to have a camera," Bess grumbled. Nancy lifted her eyebrows and shot a knowing glance at her friend. Bess's grumpy expression softened. Bess obviously wished *she* still had hers.

"Pure luck. Believe me. Like you said—how could I possibly know he'd be here?"

"You're lucky that Bruce was more interested in bundling those two out of the building than confiscating your camera," Bess remarked.

Dr. Steller looked shocked. "He'd do that?"

"Sure. He doesn't know you never had a chance to take that picture," Nancy pointed out as she started back into the theater. She stopped at the door and waited for Dr. Stars.

"Coming?"

"No point," he said. "I hate missing the start of a film—even one I've seen a dozen times. See you at the star party!" he reminded Nancy, then left.

"Some people, just because they're famous, get away with murder," Bess grumbled, catching up with Nancy.

Nancy didn't reply. She was too busy trying to figure out why she had trouble buying Dr. Stars's story.

The next day Nancy and George drove to the planetarium to read up on meteor showers in the library. Nancy had a second motive for the trip. She wanted to ferret out some information about Dr. Stars—by talking to some of the senior staff firsthand. Her run-in with him the night before at the movies had made Nancy suspect the man. Of what exactly, she had no idea—yet. But there was something shady about him, and Nancy was determined to find out what it was.

En route to the planetarium she had confided her suspicions to George, who agreed that there seemed to be more to the astronomer than met the eye.

Situated on the outskirts of town, the River Heights Planetarium was a stately old-fashioned brick building with a huge black sky dome dating from the 1930s.

But inside—it boasted state-of-the-art exhibits, including a bevy of interactive kiosks arrayed throughout the rotunda.

"Walking through here feels like walking through a maze," George remarked as they wound their way through a forest of booths. Stalls were arranged in S-shaped groups of three.

One kiosk captured Nancy's attention. "Look, George, this one on the end is all about meteors and meteor showers. Maybe we can skip the library and get our info from here." Nancy sat down in front of the display and touched the screen to start the learning program.

Definitions of *meteor, meteoroid,* and *meteorite* appeared on the monitor. "Just what Richard told us," George said, reading over Nancy's shoulder.

Using a recessed key-pad in the desktop, Nancy scrolled to the next screen. Weird electronic sounds accompanied an animated visual of a comet hurtling through space in the general direction of the Earth. A computer voice explained that meteor showers like the Perseids appear to originate from a point in space called a radiant. The location of the radiant in the sky gives the shower its name. "And this one looks like it originates in the constellation Perseus," Nancy murmured. Just as the narrator began to talk about very bright meteors called fireballs, Nancy was distracted by a vaguely familiar voice. It came from the direction of the Sky Help desk on the other side of the kiosk.

"Thank you kindly for all your help. I have always been mystified by how to read these star charts!" the familiar male voice said.

"Like I said," a woman's voice responded. "You just hold the map vertically in front of you with the direction you're facing at the bottom."

Nancy couldn't quite place the voice. "George," she said in an undertone. "Listen. Doesn't that man sound familiar?"

"And if you need any further assistance, just give me a ring. My name is Edie Washington. Here's the planetarium's information number."

"I just might do that, Ms. Washington," the man's voice fairly boomed across the spacious hall.

Sitting down, Nancy couldn't see the Sky Help desk over the S-shaped partition. So she stood up and peeked around the corner of the kiosk.

Her eyes widened, and she ducked back down. She whispered in disbelief. "You won't believe who's just lost his Texas accent!"

"What Texas accent?" George gave Nancy a puzzled look. Then, slowly, comprehension dawned on her face. "You've got to be kidding. Not Dr. Stars?"

"Dr. Stars," Nancy repeated.

10

Nabbed!

"Yo! Nancy! Did you bring your camera?" Richard yelled across the parking lot in the state park that evening. Nancy, Bess, and George had just arrived for the star party with a picnic basket.

Nancy pointed to her bag. "I've got it right here!" she yelled back as they headed to the picnic grounds.

Richard gave her a thumbs-up. "Talk to you after dinner!"

"Join us for dessert!" Nancy offered.

George chuckled, and added, "We've got some killer brownies!"

"I'll do that!" Richard promised, then returned to adjusting the mount beneath his telescope. He had set up in the vicinity of the Star Van, which Nancy noticed was still parked in the same place. A forest of telescopes seemed to have sprouted around it. Anxious star buffs hovered over their instruments, fine-tuning them for that night's viewing. Dr. Stars was there, drinking coffee from a paper cup and mixing with the crowd.

As Nancy and her friends arranged their picnic dinner on one of the wooden tables, the sun slipped below the horizon.

Nancy couldn't quite read the mood of the crowd. On the one hand, the people milling around the lot, or sprawled on blankets in the meadow, seemed to be in a party mood. But on the other hand, some of the passersby were grumbling about Dr. Stars. Last night Nancy would have defended him; tonight she wasn't so sure. Nancy directed her attention to a small group of astronomy buffs scarfing down nachos at the nearest picnic table.

"Hey, man, like I told you last night, some *real* academic must script the guy's radio shows," a redheaded man sitting with his back to Nancy declared.

One of his friends looked skeptical. "You're writing him off too soon. There's plenty of stuff he does know. Some kid was asking him about constellations, and Dr. Stars explained that though the stars *look* as though they're near enough to be connected, in fact they're light-years apart. Nothing bogus about that."

The redheaded man shrugged. "So he knows the basics—he still makes too many mistakes."

A young woman at the table suggested, "Maybe he's an expert on comets. Steller's comet is for real and he did discover it."

"Not necessarily—"

"You're not going to rehash that Derek Randall nonsense?" the woman scoffed. "That's old news. Just

81

jealousy on Randall's part. Or maybe he really believes he found the comet first, but I remember the account in *Star News* just after the discovery. Randall's report of sighting the comet came in a full twenty-four hours after Steller's."

The redheaded guy balled up his napkin and tossed it into a nearby trash basket. "Whatever. I don't need some half-baked celebrity astronomer around to help me enjoy falling stars."

As they left, Richard hurried up to Nancy's table. "Sorry to rush your dinner," he said. "But I was thinking you might want to take some pictures of the crowd before the viewing gets started."

"I figured the light would be low at best, so I put in high-speed film," Nancy told Richard. "That way I can override the flash."

Bess introduced herself and handed him a brownie while Nancy fished the camera out of her bag.

Nancy noticed he had a pair of binoculars hooked onto his belt. "Are those for stargazing?" she asked as she checked to be sure her camera was loaded. She pressed the button on the side to suppress the flash feature.

Richard shook his head. "No. They're infrared, for seeing in the dark. Hunters use them—you can pick them up at military surplus sales, pretty cheap."

"You hunt?" Bess asked with disapproval.

"No," Richard said. "But since I'm out a lot at night observing, I thought it might be fun to have these. If you're quiet enough, you can watch all sorts of nocturnal animals in the dark." He glanced at the sky. "It'll be dark soon. We'd better get started." He then suggested to Nancy, "If you don't mind, I'd feel better if you actually shoot the pictures, since it's your camera. I'll walk around with you and point out what shots would work best for the articles I'm writing."

Having already explained to her friends about helping Richard document the star party for the River Heights Astronomy Club's forthcoming newsletter, Nancy arranged to meet them as soon as she was done.

Fifteen minutes later she looked down at her camera and was surprised to see that she had only two shots left. She snapped the last two shots of cute kids in the crowd, then popped in a new roll of film. As it automatically advanced inside the camera, she complained to Richard. "But I haven't got one picture of Dr. Stars. I think he's trying to avoid me," she added, wondering if her encounter with him at the movies had made him too embarrassed to face her. She was more than eager to catch up with him, and not just to take his picture. She was curious about his sudden loss of accent at the planetarium that afternoon. Could that guy she'd overheard at dinner be right? Was Dr. Stars just a front man, an amateur astronomer and actor hired by the producers of a hit astronomy show to read a script?

"Maybe he's just camera shy," Richard remarked, gesturing to the cartoon-logo poster now set up on the hood of his van. Since the star party was an astronomy club event, Dr. Stars had dismantled his display table. He seemed to be trying to take more of a backseat tonight. "The good doctor's photogenic enough, so how come he never uses his real picture on his promotional material?"

"Believe me, I've wondered the same th

Nancy admitted wryly as she snapped a couple of pictures of Richard, then zoomed in on a white-haired man peering up at the sky through a pair of regular binoculars.

Richard tapped her shoulder. "Now's your chance to nab him," he joked. He pointed toward the trailhead where Dr. Stars stood staring into the deepening shadows of the woods. For the first time that evening no one was hanging around him. He was totally alone.

Quietly, but swiftly, Nancy circled toward him. Pushing a button to make sure her camera was on autofocus, Nancy aimed it at Dr. Stars, then called his name. "Dr. Stars!"

He turned to face her, and she clicked, the flash going off. "Oops!" Nancy winced. She had accidentally released the mechanism that was supposed to keep the flash from going off.

Dr. Stars lifted his hands to ward off the light, but it was too late. "That was totally uncalled for, Ms. Drew!" he roared. "You've just wrecked my night vision for at least twenty minutes. And why do you want my picture anyway?"

His tone was surprisingly threatening. Nancy stood her ground, but Richard spoke up before she had a chance. "Wow! You need to chill, Dr. Steller. We just wanted to take some photos for our club newsletter. Your visit to River Heights is a pretty big deal. Like, headline material."

"She's not in the club," Dr. Stars declared.

"How do you know that?" Richard wondered.

Nancy stepped in. "He knows because I told him

the other night I seldom get a chance to stargaze," she said to Richard.

"That's right. And it's pretty obvious since you don't realize that we astronomers value our night vision more than anything," Dr. Stars said, still clearly miffed.

"That's true, and Nancy had the camera on flash override." Richard turned to Nancy. "You know that most of us star watchers never use bright lights at night—even when we're camping. I never go out days without sunglasses, especially on nights I'll be observing."

Nancy tried to look apologetic, but her mind was racing. What had Richard just said about never using bright lights at night? Friday night Dr. Stars actually turned up with some super mega-watt halogen-type lantern after Derek Randall had left. Everything about Dr. Stars's behavior since that night was increasing her suspicions that he was hiding something.

"I am sorry," Nancy managed to tell him, making a mental note to rehash the events of Friday with Bess and George.

"What's done is done," Dr. Stars said in a gentler tone.

Just then a shout went up from the crowd. Nancy, Dr. Stars, and Richard all looked up at once. Everyone was pointing above their heads. There, visible to the naked eye, Nancy saw first one, then two, three, five shooting stars sailing across the northeastern quadrant of the sky.

"Awesome," George murmured, coming up behind her. "You don't even need a telescope to check out this show!"

"No—that's the beauty of it," Dr. Stars remarked. "That's the whole point of this Star Van tour."

"Could have fooled me!" someone behind Nancy mumbled loud enough for Dr. Stars to hear.

Unfazed, he went on. "You don't need lots of complicated equipment to see a really great star show—like the Perseids."

"But you use a telescope," a small boy piped up.

Dr. Stars turned and grinned at him. "That I do. But ones that aren't too complicated—that ordinary people can use with just a bit of instruction. With a telescope you can check out the craters of the moon on moonlit nights or even see the rings of Saturn."

The little boy looked impressed. Then he pointed to a red star directly overhead. "Is that Mars?"

Dr. Stars tousled the boy's hair. "You're a born astronomer. Sure, that's Mars!"

As Nancy watched, Richard's jaw dropped. "That's not Mars."

"That's Arcturus," several people chimed in.

Nancy exchanged a quick glance with George. Dr. Stars had just made another dumb mistake. What would his excuse be this time?

"Are you testing us again?" a snide voice commented from behind Nancy.

Dr. Stars looked flustered. "No, actually I wasn't. I made an honest mistake. Of course, that's not Mars. Mars isn't traversing the constellation Boötes."

"Is Arcturus a planet?" the boy asked uncertainly.

"No," Dr. Stars said firmly. "It's a star. It stays put in the sky."

"And what, I wonder, is that?" Frowning, Richard gestured toward the bluff.

Bands of red, blue, green, and purple lights were sweeping the sky.

"Floodlights!" Nancy exclaimed. "They must be coming from Woody Acres."

"That estate with all the prowlers." Dr. Stars knit his brow. "Last night their security people forced the park to illuminate all the parking areas and campsites. Tonight, colored floodlights. I should get hold of who-ever's in charge down there and tell them to cut the wattage! If they don't turn off those floodlights, we won't be able to see a thing—with or without our telescopes."

Just then Bess raced up, eyes shining. She tugged Nancy's sleeve. "Nancy—" she started to say. Then, noticing Dr. Stars nearby, she pulled Nancy out of earshot. "You won't believe it. I was looking through that telescope—and I could see Woody Acres—it's all lit up. There's a big party going on." Her voice dropped to a whisper. "I bet it has to do with you-know-who's wedding!"

Nancy grew thoughtful. She knew that a portion of the estate grounds should be visible from the over-look, but the area around the house? And people par-tying? "You can see the party from this vantage point?"

"Sure, take a look. You, too, George."

"I'll pass," George remarked, shouldering her back-pack. "Richard's moving his telescope back into the meadow. It's darker there. He said we might be able to see double stars in the constellation Lyra."

Nancy began to follow Bess when she noticed Dr.

Stars speaking on his cell phone. He clicked it shut, pocketed it, then grabbing a flashlight off the table, went down the trail into the woods.

Viewing Woody Acres would just have to wait, Nancy decided as Dr. Stars vanished into the forest. Without a second thought she hurried after the professor.

Party noises from the star watch gradually gave way to the crackly din of mid-August crickets. Otherwise the only sounds were the footsteps of Dr. Stars as he proceeded noisily down the leafy trail.

Where is he headed? Nancy asked herself. The woods thickened on either side of her, and the sweet dank smell of moldering leaves rose up from the forest floor. Pausing only to retrieve her penlight from her small leather backpack, Nancy continued to trail the astronomer. Obviously, the man had no idea he was being followed. Not only was he making no effort to walk quietly, but he had switched on his flashlight. The wedge of light it cast bounced, and Nancy found it easy to follow the beam as the path snaked gradually downward.

Abruptly the trail made a hairpin turn, then flattened out as it reached level ground. Nancy realized she was at the bottom of the hill. It was then Nancy noticed that Dr. Stars's bobbing light had vanished. Nancy froze in her tracks. Had he spotted her and turned it off? Why was it suddenly so quiet?

Holding her breath, Nancy listened. She heard only the song of crickets, the rustle of leaves as the breeze moved the branches overhead, then something small scurrying through the underbrush.

Nancy exhaled softly. Without moving she glanced first toward the dense thickets to her right, then to the overgrown banks of rhododendron bushes to her left.

All at once a branch creaked in the thicket. Nancy whirled to find herself inches from a white-tailed stag with a full rack of antlers. It gazed at her with calm, huge eyes, unfazed by her quiet presence. Then suddenly its ears pricked upward. It looked right past Nancy into the rhododendrons. With a fearful snort, it bolted back into the thicket.

The deer's acute sense of hearing had picked up the sound of something in the bushes. Something other than a small woodland creature. Something a deer would fear—a human.

Careful to step softly, Nancy turned to get a closer look at the rhododendrons; she chanced flicking her penlight back on. Dried remains of the spring blossoms were scattered among the shiny leaves. Then Nancy spied an arched opening in the tangled mass of shrubbery—it looked like a well-traveled deer path, continuing beyond the range of her penlight.

Through the natural archway Nancy heard the sound of voices. She flicked off her light and pressed herself back into the leaves. The voices were speaking hurriedly. She was too far away to make out whether the voices were male or female, or exactly how many there were or what they were saying.

Turning her penlight back on, pointing it at the ground, and keeping her head bent to avoid the branches, Nancy walked as softly as possible down the deer trail. To her amazement the trail dead-ended a few yards later against a chain-link fence.

Nancy judged that it was about ten feet high, the

top laced with spirals of razor wire. It took her only a second to figure out where she had ended up. On the northern perimeter of the Woody Acres Estate.

But what had happened to Dr. Stars? Was his one of the voices she'd heard a few minutes earlier? Nancy looked at the fence. A few feet away from where the deer trail ended, there was a hole in the fence. She tiptoed up and ran her hands carefully along the opening. The edges were smooth, not ragged. The fence wasn't broken. The wire had been deliberately cut. Whoever cut it must have set off an alarm, but the last reports of a prowler were from last night. Why hadn't the fence been fixed today?

Without a moment's hesitation, Nancy stepped right through the opening. To her right the vegetation was thick. Nancy stooped to examine the weedy scrub. The dew was thick on the greenery, and there was no sign that anyone had walked that way recently.

She proceeded to her left, keeping the fence on her left. Sure enough there was a lightly worn path, leading directly from the opening in the fence through the thinning forest.

Lights glimmered through the trees just ahead. A man stealthily edged his way along the fringe of the woods. Nancy slowed down and tried to muffle her footsteps as she trailed the man. Strains of lively salsa music drifted toward her. Soon the lights of the main house came into view, and Nancy could see the well-dressed crowd on the patio. The shadowy figure darted out of the cover of the trees and headed straight for the shelter of a gazebo.

Peering from behind a bushy, tall pine, Nancy tried

to make out the man's face. All at once she heard a footstep behind her. She whirled around, lifting her hand in a defensive karate gesture, but the sudden bright beam of a flashlight shone directly in her eyes, blinding her.

"Got you this time!" a burly voice exclaimed, and yanked her hand down, twisting her arm behind her back.

11

Stealth, Lies, Videotape

"Let go of me!" Nancy cried angrily, squirming to wriggle free.

In a single movement the man let go of her wrist and yanked off her backpack. "Hey, give me my bag!" she demanded.

"Not until I've checked it out," he told her gruffly.

"You have no right." Blinded by the glare of the flashlight, Nancy couldn't see her captor.

"Wrong. I have every right. You're trespassing on private property." Finally he redirected the light away from her face.

"Oh, Bruce, it's you!" Nancy sagged back against a tree and massaged her wrist. "Am I glad to see you!"

"You shouldn't be."

Nancy was stunned by the security guard's reaction. "Come on, Bruce, I'm not here to spy on Will Ryder. You know me."

"What I do know is that you're some kind of detective."

"Yes, I am," Nancy admitted.

"So it makes sense, doesn't it, that someone—like maybe someone from one of the tabloids—hired you to photograph the wedding, under cover, of course."

Nancy couldn't believe her ears. "You're accusing *me* of working for a tabloid and stalking Will and Isabel?" If Nancy weren't so insulted, she would have laughed.

"For all I know you're the prowler everyone's been looking for."

"That's nuts and you know it!" Nancy gasped.

Bruce didn't blink an eye. He was just a little taller than Nancy and he met her gaze steadily as he went on. "You've been conveniently in the area every time the prowler's been around."

"So were lots of other people," Nancy pointed out.

Without missing a beat, Bruce plunged ahead. "We thought it was a guy, but we never saw him up close. Maybe it was you. You were pretty handy in the woods back there—you knew exactly where someone had cut through the fence. Could it be that's because you sneaked down here and clipped the wires?"

Nancy rolled her eyes. "I'm not going to listen to one more word of this." She reached for her bag. "I'm getting out of here."

"Not with this!" Bruce held her bag above his head. He reached in and pulled out her camera and the cannister with her roll of exposed film. He shot Nancy a look of pure disgust, then shined his flashlight on her camera. "The counter says you're up to picture ten."

"Right. I took photos for the River Heights Astronomy Club newsletter this evening."

"That's a good one, Nancy Drew. Do you think I was born yesterday?" he scoffed. "I bet if I developed this role the prints would have nothing to do with star parties, and everything to do with a certain movie star." Bruce shot Nancy a look of pure disgust. "I saw you and your friend Bess at the movies last night, stalking Mr. Ryder. Couldn't she wait until we replaced her camera? Did she rush out and buy another one while Mr. Ryder was still in town? Or did she just use yours?" He shook the camera in the air.

"I saw you at the movies, too," Nancy charged. "But you fell down on the job, Bruce. Bob Steller was the one with the camera last night. Not us."

Bruce narrowed his eyes. "You're trying to tell me that Dr. Stars was taking pictures of Will Ryder?" He laughed. "Gimme a break."

"It's the truth. He left the star party, and I followed him to someplace near the fence. But I'm sure I just saw him moving toward the gazebo." She turned toward the gazebo. What she saw made her jaw drop. Dr. Stars was indeed in the gazebo, but he was in full view, talking animatedly with Carlos Ramos, owner of Woody Acres.

"What's he doing?" Nancy exclaimed.

"Complaining. Like he's been doing ever since he came to River Heights. He doesn't like the lights down here—he thinks we're trying to jinx his star tour," Bruce said, sounding vaguely annoyed. "He's certainly not *stalking* anyone, though he's been as much trouble as any fan, as far as I'm concerned. If

Marie hasn't escorted him off the property by the time I'm through with you, I will. Believe me."

Nancy didn't know how to respond. "But I did follow him through the woods," she insisted.

"Interesting story. Sorry to inform you that whoever you followed through the woods wasn't Dr. Stars. He turned up at the front gate a little while ago. Beats me how he got there."

But the man she followed *was* Dr. Stars. Nancy was sure of that. Still, Bruce could be partially right. The blacktopped north park road ran parallel to the forest path Nancy had just traveled. Had the doctor headed down the path toward the road and gotten a ride to Woody Acres? His van *was* more or less hemmed in by the telescope crowd, but he could have asked someone for a ride.

Nancy let out a frustrated sigh. She felt as if she were standing in the middle of a jigsaw puzzle, with too few pieces to fill in the blanks. She was not at all ready to accept Bruce's explanation about Dr. Stars. Still, at the moment, what she needed to do was safely retrieve her camera.

"Look, Bruce," she said, "just give me back my camera and bag and I'll leave."

"You bet you'll leave," he replied. "Stop by the office Tuesday, after the wedding's over, you'll get your camera back, minus the film."

"But, Bruce, those pictures, they're for the—"

"I know. The newsletter," he scoffed. "Tell the newsletter folks that they'll have to print without pictures, or to draw some." He began to search Nancy's bag, but she snatched it, and zipped it shut.

"You've got my camera—not that you have any real right to it—but you have no right to go through this bag. If you do I'm calling my father. He's a lawyer and knows your boss very well—"

"I know your father, too," Bruce tossed back, but he didn't try to retrieve Nancy's bag. Instead he guided her back to the hole in the fence, and made her go through it, back into the forest.

"I'm sure you know your way from here," he said with exaggerated sweetness.

Nancy gritted her teeth and headed back up the deer path through the rhododendron bushes. She turned back, to see Bruce standing there, watching her.

She retraced her steps and slogged back up to the star party. It was late, but the crowd had barely thinned out. In fact to Nancy's eye it looked like more of the astronomy club had hit the scene.

"Nancy! Where were you?" Bess cried, hurrying down the trail from the parking lot. George was right behind her.

"I'm not sure you want to know," Nancy said, sinking heavily onto a bench. The climb up the path had been steep. Now the muscles in her legs were aching, and her shoulder smarted from where Bruce had twisted her arm. She quickly checked her bag, pulling out her wallet, her hairbrush, her notebook, and her makeup case. Everything was there. Bruce had only confiscated the film and the camera.

When she looked up at Bess, she slowly grinned, as she put her things back in her bag. "On the other hand, you'll love to hear this." Nancy filled the cousins in on following Dr. Stars, losing him in the woods, the hole in the Woody Acres fence, and finally her unpleasant encounter with Bruce.

"I can't believe he accused you of spying!" George was indignant. "Especially with Dr. Stars lurking around."

"But like Nancy said, he wasn't lurking at all. Still, why go through those creepy woods just to complain to Mr. Ramos?" Bess shuddered.

George scoffed, "This from the girl who'd do any-thing to get close to Will Ryder—would you let a mere forest filled with wild terrible beasts keep you from your heartthrob?"

Bess giggled. "No." Then she sighed. "Too bad it got dark so fast. While there was still light I could almost make out the people down at the estate by looking through those big stargazing binoculars."

Nancy felt a sudden surge of energy. "Bess," she said, jumping up and giving Bess a hug. "Did you just say binoculars?"

Bess nodded.

"I've got an idea, and you might get a chance to get a good close look at your hero." She scanned the crowd. With the exception of some carefully shaded camping lanterns and penlights, the area was dark. "Have you seen Richard?" she asked Bess and George.

"Yeah, he's over with the group from the astronomy club." George motioned toward Dr. Stars's van.

Without waiting for George to finish, Nancy wended her way through the crowd. "Richard," she said, "I need to talk to you."

"Did you finish with the pictures? You want to give me the roll, and I'll get them developed?"

Nancy winced. "Uh—about the pictures, can I talk to you about them tomorrow?"

Richard looked puzzled. "Sure."

"At the moment what I need is to borrow your binoculars—those infrared ones." Nancy pointed to the pair hanging from his belt.

Richard unhooked them and handed them over.

"Can I keep them until tomorrow?"

"No problem," he said. "Or any time next week you're near the shop, just drop in and return them. I'm in no rush for them."

"Thanks!" Nancy said, then went to retrieve a regular flashlight from her car.

A few minutes later she was heading back into the forest. This time Bess and George were with her. Nancy took the lead, Bess tried to stick close behind her, while George brought up the rear. With the help of the flashlight, they made quick progress down the trail.

When Nancy judged they'd gone about halfway, she cut off the path and turned left toward the border of the estate. Because the land was higher and drier this far up the hill, no rhododendron bushes clogged the forest floor. But the hill was still steep, and the going was slow and noisy. Though, as Bess pointed out, at least the racket would keep anything wild and carnivorous away.

Soon they arrived at the fence hemming in the estate. Nancy switched off her flashlight and warned the two other girls to keep their voices low. Nancy had calculated correctly. On the Woody Acres side of the fence the forest gave way to a broad expanse of lawn. From the shelter of the trees, Nancy could see that the party was still in full swing.

Bess swayed her body gently in time to the rhythm of the dance music drifting toward them. "What I wouldn't give to crash that party!"

"Nothing's stopping you," George teased softly. "Except a couple of really bad-tempered security guards and barbed wire mean enough to rip a hole in your leg, even if you could manage to climb such a high fence."

"Keep your voices down," Nancy reminded them, unhooking the binoculars from her belt.

"Are we close enough to see faces?" Bess asked eagerly as Nancy popped off the lens caps covering each eyepiece.

"You tell me," Nancy said, handing the binoculars over to Bess. No harm in letting Bess check out the party first.

Bess aimed them at the crowd dancing on the pool deck, then adjusted the focusing knob. "Things look definitely weird."

"That's because they're infrared," Nancy told her.

"They're pretty powerful," Bess remarked. "I can make out people's faces. But I don't see *him*," she moaned.

"Who, Dr. Stars?" George asked, feigning innocence.

"No—Will, silly!" Bess countered, continuing to look through the binoculars. "Now, that's really strange," she remarked suddenly. "You'd think Marie would notice that astronomy guy."

"Marie's there—and she can see Dr. Stars?" Nancy questioned, and reached for the binoculars.

As Bess handed them over, she shook her head. "Not Dr. Stars, the other one. The older man."

"Derek!" Nancy gasped, peering through the binoculars. Holding a cocktail in one hand, the astronomer was casually mingling with the other guests. "I don't get it. How did he wheedle himself into this party?"

"What's his game, Nancy?" George asked. "He's supposedly on some camping trip and just happens to run into his arch rival—or almost run into him. Now he turns up at a glamorous party that's not at all the astronomy scene."

"Tell me about it," Nancy said, continuing to carefully scan the partygoers with the binoculars. Except for Derek Randall, she didn't see anyone she recognized—not even Mr. Ramos or Will Ryder or his fiancée. She widened her search, checking out the vicinity near the mansion itself. Dark shrubbery hugged the side of the sprawling two-story wooden house. Suddenly a furtive movement caught Nancy's eye. A figure darted from behind a clump of bushes near the gazebo, ducking quickly behind a potted palm. As Nancy watched, the figure straightened up. "I don't believe this!" she gasped. "Bruce said he or Marie was going to escort Dr. Stars off the premises. But he's still at the party."

"Maybe Mr. Ramos invited him to stay," Bess suggested. "To smooth stuff out because of all the lights and ruining his star lecture and the comet viewing tonight."

"Then why," Nancy asked, "is he hiding in the bushes, videotaping the party!"

12

A Clever Trail

The next morning Nancy woke up with the vivid image of Dr. Stars holding the videocamera fresh in her mind. No question he was stalking Will Ryder. But why? Stars was a famous and successful astronomer, a public personality. So public, Nancy reflected, that he probably disguised his Texas accent at the planetarium the day before, just so he wouldn't be recognized. Though why he would play dumb about a star chart was beyond Nancy, unless he was just an actor for the show.

No matter what, stalking a movie star seemed way out of his line of expertise. What could be his motive?

As Nancy padded down the hall to the shower, the answer seemed obvious—greed. Tabloid TV shows would probably pay mega-bucks for footage of the ultra-private prewedding party of one of Hollywood's A-list stars.

It was almost as obvious that Protection and Detection security guard Marie Russo was in cahoots with him. Bruce had told Nancy that Marie was going to escort Dr. Stars off the grounds. Yet an hour later he was still at the party—stealthily taping the event. Nancy could picture a scenario: After Bob Steller's irate conversation with the estate owner, Marie would have made a big deal of marching him off toward the gate. Then, when no one was looking, she'd let him go.

As for the videocamera itself, Nancy realized it was small enough to fit easily into one of the many pockets of the astronomer's vest.

But what about Derek Randall? What was his connection to the whole deal? Nancy couldn't stop wondering if somehow the famous rivalry between the two astronomers was a fraud. That maybe they were in cahoots.

Unable to shake the feeling that the missing clue was right under her nose, Nancy decided to review the facts she'd jotted down in her notebook over breakfast. Nancy showered, then dressed in her favorite broken-in pair of jeans and a three-quarter-sleeve T-shirt. She clattered downstairs and went right to the little table in the foyer to get the notebook from her bag. She unzipped the small backpack, but the notebook wasn't there.

"Hannah?" she asked, walking into the kitchen with her bag in her hand. "Have you seen my notebook?"

"No, Nancy. Did you have it with you last night?" the Drews' housekeeper inquired as she poured Nancy a cup of coffee.

"I'm pretty sure I did," Nancy said, "but I honestly can't remember when I last saw it."

"Maybe some breakfast will jog your memory," Hannah suggested, putting a bowl of fruit on the table and handing Nancy a basket of fresh blueberry muffins. As she ate, Nancy tried to recall when she last saw her little notebook. It was in her bag when she took out her penlight to help trail Dr. Stars the night before. Bruce had pulled her camera out of the small backpack, but when Nancy had retrieved the bag she saw the blue cover of the notebook before she zipped it back up.

"Oh, I remember!" Nancy suddenly recollected what had happened. After her nasty encounter with Bruce, she'd met up with Bess and George in the meadow. Stopping at one of the picnic tables, she'd checked the contents of her bag. She'd taken out her notebook and had probably forgotten to put it back in. "Hannah, I bet I left it on one of the picnic tables up at the star watch last night."

Nancy finished breakfast, helped Hannah with some of the morning's chores, then left for the state park. Though it was a perfect summer day with a warm stiff breeze, Nancy arrived at the day use area to find it nearly deserted. Dr. Stars's van was still parked near the embankment, but the astronomer was nowhere in sight. Where did he keep going without his van? Nancy could swear it looked as though it hadn't been moved in days. But except for a couple of minivans and a nondescript midsize yellow car, the lot was empty. It *was* a weekday, Nancy reflected as she locked her Mustang and trotted across the pavement to the deserted picnic area.

To her relief she spotted her notebook right away. It was lying on the wooden bench of a table shaded by a tall leafy oak. Nancy sat on the edge of the bench and checked her notes. Up here on the high point of the park, the breeze was gusting, and Nancy had to hold down the pages. Quickly she skimmed the lists of facts she'd jotted down about Dr. Stars's van, his journal, Derek Randall's brusque behavior, and pointers on stargazing she'd gleaned from Richard. Nothing shed light on any possible connection between Derek Randall and Dr. Stars.

Just as she was despairing of learning anything new from her notes, some folded sheets of paper slipped out of the back of the book. The wind caught at them and sent them fluttering through the goldenrod. Nancy jumped to retrieve them. When she unfolded them, she realized she had never really read them before. They were printouts of the first couple of pages of Dr. Stars's Web site. "I forgot all about this stuff," she murmured. As she read the biographical information on the first sheet, her eyes widened. "I can't believe I skipped over all this." Not only was Bob Steller an only child, but his birth date made him close to fifty.

The Bob Steller who gave the star talks wasn't even thirty. Nancy was sure of that, just as she was sure he had been lying about taking snapshots of Will Ryder for his kid sister. The real Dr. Stars had no sister.

Nancy stared at the page only for a second, then jumped up and jogged over to the Star Van. It was locked, the back and side curtains drawn. Shading her eyes from the sun, Nancy peered through the windshield. No one was inside.

She stared out at the valley below. In daylight, except for the glint of sun on the mansard roof and the long swath of blacktopped driveway that cut through the trees, it was hard to see much of the house at Woody Acres. Still, Nancy knew enough about cameras to realize that super-powerful telescopic lenses could easily pick out details of face and dress on people congregated on the estate grounds below. Tomorrow night, if Bess's information was right, was the wedding. The man impersonating Dr. Stars was sure to be here illegally documenting the proceedings, while masquerading as a stargazer.

So who was the imposter? Nancy decided that she didn't have time to worry about that now. The more urgent question was, where was the real Dr. Stars? Every instinct told Nancy he was in some kind of big-time trouble. The fake Dr. Stars would have had to get rid of the real Bob Steller, one way or another.

Nancy's blood ran cold. He'd probably been kidnapped.

For a moment Nancy was stymied. Whatever had happened to Dr. Stars had happened—at the latest—Friday night. Nancy referred to her notebook. Friday was the night that the astronomer's journal entries had stopped; Thursday night was when his wife had last heard from him.

And this is Monday, Nancy realized with a sinking heart. If Bob Steller was abducted, the trail would already be cold. Nancy's thoughts tumbled wildly in her head. First thing she decided to do was notify the police—she didn't have much to go on, but the discrepancies between Dr. Stars's bio and whoever was running the star lectures would be enough for the police to believe that Nancy was on to something. At the same time Nancy might be able to find out whatever happened to the prowler the cops were tracking Friday night. Could he have been the fake Dr. Stars?

As she reached in her bag for her cell phone, a gust of wind blew Nancy's notebook off the hood of the van. She hurried after it, snatching it up at the curb bordering the picnic area. As she straightened up, something black and shiny caught her eye. Caught in the metal work of a storm drain on the parking lot pavement was a round black plastic object. Curious, Nancy pried it out. The two-inch-wide circle of plastic was attached to a threaded flat-ended screw. It looked like some kind of focusing knob. Nancy examined it more closely. Along the edge was etched the word Starfield. That was the brand name of Dr. Stars's telescope—the one missing the knob.

Excitement mounted in Nancy. "Cool it!" she warned herself. After all, there had been two gatherings of astronomers at this site over the past two nights—with dozens of telescopes, probably half of them the popular Starfield brand. Anyone could have lost a focusing knob.

Nancy put the knob in her bag, and then noticed something white fluttering in the weeds just a few feet away, right at the start of the trailhead. Bending down, she saw it was a small sheet of paper, sticking out of a cardboard dispenser packet. The piece of paper was lens paper; the brand name was Starfield.

Nancy held the packet a moment and just stared at it. Funny it should turn up just a few feet from the knob. Intuition propelled Nancy a little farther down the path. She felt as though there had to be something else. She didn't even know if the knob and the packet were clues or just bits of garbage. Just then Nancy spied something slim, round, and black lying just to the side of the path. She pounced on it. A lens cap.

Each object she'd found so far had lain conveniently along the side of the trail, as if deliberately dropped. She kept her eyes glued to the ground and proceeded another couple of yards down the trail. Right before she entered the woods, her foot struck something small and hard. Nancy looked down. Half-hidden by a small rock was the silvery shaft of a key. Nancy moved the rock, to discover the key was one of three on a hard rubber key ring, molded into the shape of a telescope.

"Like Hansel and Gretel leaving a trail of crumbs," she murmured. She was ninety-nine percent sure now. Someone had dropped this stuff on purpose. Was it the real Dr. Stars?

Shoving her sunglasses on top of her head, Nancy followed the trail into the woods. Shafts of sunlight dappled the forest floor. By daylight Nancy could see that the trail branched in three directions. Wooden trail marker arrows were nailed into a broad tree trunk: one was painted white, one fluorescent red, one a garish safety orange.

Nancy recognized the white trail, which was broad and straight, as the one she'd traveled the night before. The red trail curved off to the left; the orange to the right. Wishing she had a trail map, Nancy stood perplexed. Studying the ground again, she saw some tissues, a couple of soda cans, and a beer bottle. Overhead, leaves rustled as the branches swayed in the breeze. Patterns of sunlight shifted, and for a second Nancy thought she saw something glitter on the ground where the rockier orange path started. The light shifted, leaving the area dark. Nancy dropped to one knee and examined the ground, running her hand gently over the carpet of moldy leaves. Her fingers touched something cold and metal. A ring! Nancy brushed off the dirt, and held the plain gold band up to the light. Inscribed inside were the initials RS & TS and the word "Forever."

The *R* puzzled Nancy for just a second before she got it: *R* stood for *Robert*. "Robert Steller and Teresa Steller!" It was the real Dr. Stars's wedding band, and he had dropped it. Now Nancy was positive he was purposely leaving a trail in the hope that someone would eventually come looking for him: the focusing knob, the lens paper, the lens cap, the keys. Ah, the keys, Nancy thought. They did look familiar. Examining them again she realized they were car keys, probably to the van, which explained why the fake Dr. Stars hadn't moved it.

This last clue, the wedding band, clinched it. Dr. Stars had left her just the clue Nancy needed to find him. She hurried down the sloping, rocky path. Within a quarter of a mile it ended abruptly in a clearing at the base of a steep cliff. A stream flowed by on Nancy's left. To her right she spied one of the park's hunting cabins.

During the summer, cabins this far back in the woods seldom found renters, though the waiting list for weekly rentals during the fall hunting season was long. So Nancy was surprised to see that the door of the cabin was open and creaking slightly in the breeze. Maybe a park cleanup crew was readying the cabin for winter. Still, the trail of Dr. Stars's clues had definitely led in this direction.

Taking a deep breath, Nancy cautiously backed up until she was under cover of the trees. Careful not to break even a twig under foot, Nancy approached the cabin from the side. The windows were shuttered. Bending low, she scurried across the tiny yard and crouched behind the open door. She listened for voices. After a moment she realized there were none.

Stealthily she stepped inside. Dust was thick on the table and chairs. Cobwebs festooned the corners and the opening to a fireplace. The place looked as if no one had been there for nearly a year. Nancy stepped farther inside. Dust rose up with each step. Suddenly she stopped in her tracks. Someone *had* been here. A trail of footprints crisscrossed the floor. They were messy and Nancy couldn't tell much from them. Only that the cabin had been used lately, and that the footprints led to the table and to a pile of what looked like photo and video equipment in a corner. Nancy proceeded to examine the gear. It was an impressive array: several tripods were propped against the wall. A videocamera was on one of the chairs. An open black nylon camera bag revealed a couple of digital cameras. Everything looked cutting edge, top of the line, and extremely professional.

Behind Nancy the door squeaked. Thinking it was the wind, she didn't turn. Suddenly a shadow blossomed on the wall in front of her. Before Nancy could react, she felt something slam hard against her head. Her legs crumpled under her, and she collapsed to the floor, hitting her forehead against the chair. She fought to keep her eyes open, but everything began to fog over. The last sounds she heard were a door slamming and a bolt being jammed shut.

13

Friend or Foe?

"Wake up! Please!" The words seeped into Nancy's consciousness. The voice was vaguely familiar. Nancy drifted back to sleep, wondering to whom it belonged. Who'd be trying to wake her up? Not George. Not Bess. Not Hannah. Then she felt something cold and wet falling on her face.

She tried to speak, but only a low moan worked its way through her lips. Where was she anyway? Had she fallen asleep somewhere, in the rain? Nancy struggled to open her eyes, but as she moved her head she was sickened by a sudden searing pain.

Someone shook her shoulder. Then she felt more water dripping on her face. "What . . ." she gasped as she managed to force her eyes open. Her eyelids felt like little bricks. Nancy tried to move again, but she felt as if a ten-ton elephant were stomping on her head.

"Oh." The voice breathed a sigh of relief. "You're all right!"

"Not exactly." Nancy woozily tried to sit up. Strong hands against her back eased her into a sitting position. Nancy blinked and slowly looked around the room. All at once everything came back to her—the walk from the parking lot, the trail of clues, the empty cabin. Head still throbbing, Nancy snapped right back into full consciousness—and gasped.

"You!" she cried, horrified to see Marie Russo kneeling in front of her, a bandanna in her hand. The blue-and-white cloth was dripping with water. She was wearing her shirt with the Protection and Detection logo; apparently she was on duty. Nancy tried to stand up, to get out of her reach.

She struggled to her feet, but her knees seemed to turn to mush. As Nancy began to sway, Marie jumped up, grabbed her around the waist, and steadied her.

Every instinct made Nancy want to get away from Marie, but she was powerless. The blow to her head had left her shaky. Nancy would have to bide her time. At the moment she had no choice but to let Marie ease her into one of the straight-backed wooden chairs beside the table.

Nancy kept her eye on the guard, half expecting her to pull out handcuffs, to take her prisoner. Strands of long red curls had escaped from Marie's braid. Her naturally pale complexion had gone almost dead white. Nancy realized that the large green eyes staring at her were terrified.

"Stop looking at me that way," Marie snapped, her

harsh tone barely masking the fear in her voice. "What are you doing here anyway?"

"What am *I* doing here?" Nancy repeated in disbelief. "In case you hadn't noticed, this isn't Woody Acres property. This is a public park. More like, what are *you* doing here? Guarding all this equipment?" Nancy added sarcastically.

Marie glared at Nancy. Tossing her braid over her shoulder, she planted her hands on her hips and said incredulously, "You think *I* have something to do with this stuff?"

"Looks that way. I came in here. I checked out the equipment, and next thing I know you're standing over me—"

"Sprinkling water on your face. Come off it. Why would I bop you on the head, lock the door on both of us from the *outside,* then try to bring you around?"

"The door's bolted?" Nancy vaguely recalled the sound of the door slamming. Now she straightened up and rubbed her head. She stood and, brushing Marie's hand aside, walked slowly to the door, fighting to keep her balance. She tried the latch. It didn't budge.

"Testing me?" Marie challenged snidely.

"What do you expect?" Nancy turned and shot a scathing glance at Marie. Meanwhile, Nancy continued to pace the floor slowly, kneading the back of her neck with her hand. With every step she felt less dizzy, more surefooted. She decided that she'd get what information she could from Marie. But at the same time she'd been examining her surroundings, looking for a way out. "So what *are* you doing here then?"

Marie studied Nancy before answering. "I don't

know why I should trust you, but since we're both in the same boat here, I guess we might as well be on the same side."

Nancy folded her arms across her chest and eyed Marie coldly. "Meaning we're both locked in—"

"Meaning we both came here looking for something." Marie leaned back against the table, and with one finger doodled absently in the dust as she spoke. "I was patrolling the perimeter of Woody Acres, checking to see if that hole in the fence Bruce had reported had been mended."

At the mention of the fence Nancy shook her head. "I bet it wasn't."

Marie laughed. "Good guess! Anyway, as I approached I heard something in the bushes on the other side of the fence. I looked through and caught a glimpse of some guy hurrying up the hill toward the main path. He turned—I didn't think he saw me—but now I'm sure he did. Anyway, it was that Dr. Stars person."

"Let me guess," Nancy said. "You followed him here."

"Yes. I hid outside in the bushes while he went inside. The windows are shuttered, so I couldn't see what he was up to. Then suddenly he came out again and headed back toward Woody Acres. I wasn't sure if I should follow him back there or check the cabin. I decided Bruce could deal with him if he turned up at the estate, so I came in here and found the same stuff you did. All this photography equipment. I opened the camera bag, hoping to find some ID inside, when I heard someone skulking outside the front door. I ducked into the bedroom back there and closed the door. I couldn't see out, but the person I heard must have been you. Then I heard something fall, the door slam, and the bolt being thrown shut. Whoever knocked you out must have been following you pretty closely."

Nancy couldn't deny that Marie's explanation made sense, though she still had too many unanswered questions to trust the woman completely. "Did you figure out who this equipment belongs to?"

Marie shook her head. "It's high-grade professional stuff," she said as Nancy picked up one of the cameras and looked through the powerful telescopic lens. "I thought it might belong to Dr. Stars, but then why would an astronomer have all these high-end cameras? And why stash them here, rather than in his van?" Marie chewed at the end of her braid. "I hate to say this, but I have a feeling Bruce might be involved in all of this somehow. Maybe this stuff doesn't belong to the astronomer at all. Maybe it's Bruce's."

Silently Nancy agreed, but she wasn't ready to share her suspicions about Bruce with Marie. Or that she'd had her own rather difficult encounter with him the night before. Part of her wanted to trust Marie. Another part couldn't forget the way Marie had acted toward Bess—and that it was Marie who was supposed to escort the fake Bob Steller off the estate the night before.

Nancy decided to test the waters. Straddling a chair, she asked Marie, "Wouldn't it be weird if Dr. Stars was an imposter?"

Marie made a face. "You mean, someone is pretending to be Dr. Stars?" She paused and shrugged. "Like why?"

"I don't know for sure except, in case you hadn't noticed, if you're looking through a telescope near where his van is parked, there's a pretty good view of Woody Acres: the pool, the deck, the lawn area— even the tennis courts."

As Nancy watched, comprehension slowly dawned on Marie's thin face. She slapped her hand on the top of the table. "Of course. A paparazzo! They get such big bucks that that's motive enough for someone to take a chance to pose as Dr. Stars."

"You must have suspected something. You were up there Saturday night at Dr. Stars's lecture," Nancy reminded her.

"I was. I mean, I did. But only after I got up there. I had seen the flyer for the star lecture, and I've always been sort of interested in astronomy. But when I got to the lecture and saw that it overlooked Woody Acres, I began to suspect that someone in that crowd might be trying to spy on Will Ryder. Actually"— Marie looked embarrassed—"it was Bruce who raised my suspicions. The night the prowler was at Woody Acres, I was sure I saw a guy who resembled Dr. Stars walking down the north road when I was driving to work. I mentioned this to Bruce, and he acted all weird. Then Saturday afternoon I saw him talking to Dr. Stars, and when Bruce saw me, he tried to pretend he was just giving the guy directions."

"So when Bruce spotted you at the star party, he must have suspected that you were on to him," Nancy theorized.

"I don't know," Marie admitted.

"It's hard to put all the pieces together," Nancy said. Then she told Marie about running into Dr. Stars taking pictures of Will at the movie theater, and that he also was sneaking around the estate the night before, taping the prewedding party.

"But I escorted him off the premises," Marie protested, shocked. "He couldn't have sneaked back in!"

"Not without help," Nancy pointed out.

"Bruce," Marie sounded disappointed. "I had hoped I was wrong about him."

"But the person I can't place in all of this," Nancy told her, "is Derek Randall. He's Bob Steller's arch rival. I can't figure out what role he's playing here."

"Mr. Randall?" Marie looked confused. "He doesn't fit in at all—I mean, he's here for the wedding."

"Will Ryder and Isabel Ramos-Garcia's wedding? You've got to be kidding." Try as she might, Nancy couldn't for the life of her picture the arrogant academic astronomer hanging out with Will Ryder's crowd.

"Derek Randall is related to Isabel through marriage. She's his wife's niece," Marie explained. "He's a guest at the estate. Besides, I think he teaches at Grimsley College where Will Ryder went for a while. Someone told me he introduced them. Maybe that's just a rumor," Marie conjectured, then flashed a wicked smile at Nancy. "Your blond friend—she's a fan—she probably has the scoop on every detail of Mr. Ryder's life!"

Nancy returned Marie's grin. "I'll ask her—that is, if we ever get out of here." Nancy shrugged. "So I guess that explains why Randall was in the area, and it makes sense that while he was here he'd check out the local astronomy scene." Nancy wanted to kick herself for rushing to judgment on Derek Randall. All along he'd been suspicious of Dr. Stars.

"But, Nancy"—Marie's worried voice interrupted Nancy's thoughts—"who is posing as Dr. Stars? And where's the real Bob Steller?"

14

Time Runs Out

"I was hoping the real Dr. Stars would be in this cabin," Nancy answered grimly.

She went on to explain to Marie how she had followed the trail of clues dropped by the astronomer. "This cabin is so off the main hiking path, I thought someone might have hidden him here. Obviously he isn't in that back room?"

Marie shook her head. "No. Except for a rolled-up mattress and more dust, the bedroom's empty."

Nancy decided to have a look for herself. The cabin's sleeping quarters were sparsely furnished: a plain metal bedstead, a painted wooden night table that had seen better days, and the rolled-up mattress on top of the bed. There were no closets, no cupboards, nowhere for a person to hide—or be hidden, Nancy realized. She felt frustrated, having come all this way and hitting another dead end.

While Marie walked around the room, trying to open the shutters, Nancy looked more closely at the bed. Gingerly she rolled the mattress over, exposing more of the bed frame springs. Beneath the bed she spied a short piece of rope. Another piece was knotted around one of the bedposts. The ends had been cut. "Marie—he *was* here, after all. Look at this!" Nancy said, holding up a piece of rope. "And whoever moved him was in a rush. They didn't bother to unknot the rope."

Marie's worried frown deepened as she looked at the rope. "What good does that do us, Nancy? We're stuck in here, and we still don't know what happened to him."

"Except," Nancy said, trying to look on the bright side, "that he was alive when he was here. If someone wanted to do away with him permanently, they wouldn't have bothered to tie him up, and then move him." Nancy strode back into the main room, Marie right behind her. "But where is he now? Where would someone move him?"

"Wait—" Marie suddenly cried. She stared at Nancy. "I just remembered something. I can't believe I've been so stupid. I was so worried about you—it took so long to wake you up—that I totally forgot."

Nancy gripped the young woman's forearm. "Forgot what, Marie?"

Marie put her hands on her temples and closed her eyes a moment. "Let's see. I was in the back room. I heard that thud in here. Then the cabin door closed, and I heard someone throw the bolt. I rushed out and nearly tripped over you. When you didn't come to right away, I went to my backpack for my water bottle. That's when I overheard him . . ."

"Who?"

"I don't know *who*, but it was a man right outside talking to someone. I tried to peek out of the shutters, but they're fitted too snugly—I couldn't see a thing. But I heard this man—at first I thought he was with another person—but I heard him say, 'Can you make it to the shed in an hour? Me, too. See you there then,' and then I heard something click."

"Like a cell phone?" Nancy suggested.

"Exactly."

"Marie, is there a shack around here?"

"No—I mean, not that I know of. Besides, why would it take someone an hour to get to someplace near here? He said a shed rather than a cabin—the only place there'd be all sorts of outbuildings and sheds is where the park's maintenance equipment is kept. That's right near the entrance, only a thirty-minute slow hike."

"You've got a point there," Nancy conceded. "That rules out the park. But did he say anything else? Think, Marie. Even if it doesn't seem important, it might be a clue."

Marie started to shake her head, then her face lit up. "Wait, I do remember something else. Something about scratching the plan, and moving the old guy—he also said something about an observatory and a parking lot."

"There's no observatory within an hour of here," Nancy mused, then brightened. "Unless he meant the planetarium." Nancy squeezed Marie's shoulder. "That's it. The River Heights Planetarium. The fake Dr. Stars knows exactly where that is. I saw him there a couple of days ago myself. If you push the speed limit and take back roads, it's just about an hour away."

"Who's the old guy?"

Nancy managed a small smile. "The genuine Dr. Stars. I doubt he'd call himself old. He's about Derek Randall's age."

Marie eyed Nancy skeptically. "Then how did the fake Dr. Stars think he'd pull that off? He's about my age."

"I guess he counted on not running into anyone who'd ever seen Dr. Stars in person. After all, he is a radio personality—it's not like someone would know his face from TV or anything. And," Nancy added, "he is good at accents. Whoever he is, that imposter's quite an actor."

"An actor?" Marie repeated, staring hard at Nancy. "Wait a minute." Marie sagged against the door. "That's it! I'm pretty sure who's posing as Dr. Stars." She gave a resigned sigh. "And I'm more than sure Bruce is part of the scam!" Marie hesitated before saying more. Nancy wanted to shake her. Didn't she realize that solving this mystery meant possibly saving Dr. Stars's life?

"The other day at the office, Mr. Korinthenos was out when this fax came through. I picked it up—it was from one of our associate agencies on the West Coast—in L.A., actually. It was about Jake Mc-Curdy—he's one of the most notorious paparazzi in the biz. He'll stop at nothing to get a story—photos, bribes to hired help. His clients hire him, pay him mega-bucks up front to snare an exclusive, and they turn the other way when he pushes the envelope and breaks the law."

"So what did the fax say?" Nancy prodded.

"I only saw the first page. It was enough. Some source said he was in this area to scoop Mr. Ryder's wedding."

"But what makes you think he's the fake Dr. Stars, Marie? I mean, the guy could be hanging around— maybe he's even your prowler, but how did he fake Dr. Stars?"

"Easy. The guy's an actor. I don't know a whole lot about him except that he started out in Hollywood, trying his hand at the biz. Then he worked for a while as a stuntman."

"Then he can probably fake accents," Nancy said.

"I'm sure he can. He seems to be able to disguise himself when he wants to. And who knows what he really looks like—thanks to Bruce."

"What's Bruce got to do with it?"

"He was there in the office when the fax started transmitting. I picked up the first page. More pages came through as I was reading, but before I could pick them up, Bruce grabbed the stuff. He said something about phoning Mr. K. right away to say we'd been put on alert. But before he walked off with the papers, I noticed one had a picture on it. Not that I got to look at it—I just saw there was a photo," she admitted glumly.

"Of course not. Bruce made sure of that. He couldn't afford for you to recognize McCurdy when you ran into Dr. Stars," Nancy concluded. "I've got to give McCurdy credit," she went on. "He had everyone fooled. His accent was perfect. The only time I heard him drop it was at the planetarium when he probably didn't want the person at the desk to think he was a famous astronomer asking very amateur questions. Too bad all those astronomy buffs in the club wrote Dr. Stars off as just a bad astronomer."

"What do you mean?" Marie inquired.

Nancy shrugged. "The real Dr. Stars probably knows his astronomical facts cold. This McCurdy guy made so many gaffs he should have been spotted as a fake." Nancy forced herself to stop thinking about McCurdy. "Look, Marie. We can worry about all this later. Right now we have to get out of here and to the planetarium."

Marie shook her head. "I've tried the door, the shutters . . . it's no use. They just won't budge."

"I usually have something in my bag—a penknife, something that might work open that lock." Nancy looked around before spotting her bag in front of the fireplace. It was open and the contents were scattered on the floor. Her makeup case lay half in the ashes on the grate; her notebook was under the andirons; pens, pencils, and a couple of scrunchies for her hair had fallen under the table. Fortunately so had her car keys. Bruce or McCurdy—whichever one had attacked her and made off with her wallet—hadn't found the keys. "They probably took the wallet so I wouldn't have a credit card to try to work open the locks," Nancy complained bitterly. She dusted off her stuff and put it back in her bag, looping a scrunchie around her wrist. With all the shutters and the door closed, the cabin was sweltering in the midday heat.

"Is that a cell phone?" Marie pointed toward the wood box. A small flip-top phone was half hidden in the shadows. Marie retrieved it and handed it to Nancy.

Nancy punched a couple of buttons and held the phone to her ear, then made a face. "It's broken."

"You sound good at all this breaking and entering," Marie marveled.

Nancy chuckled. "Bruce probably forgot to tell you, but I do a bit of detecting myself, and I generally can get out of tight places. This, however, is a bit of a challenge. How about *your* bag? Anything promising inside?"

"I looked already—*nada*," Marie said. "Just my lunch, the water I used to help you come round, and a book. My personal stuff—wallet, all that—is in a closet back at Woody Acres. I don't like to carry too much personal ID on the job." She paused. "But I do have an idea. How strong are you?"

Nancy smiled and made a muscle with her arm. "Karate; some judo; I've even tried boxing—why?"

Impressed, Marie let out a low whistle. "Great! Between the two of us we can try to ram our way out of here. The sideboards on the bed frame are heavy and strong. I couldn't manage on my own, but with you . . ."

Nancy instantly caught her drift. She and Marie went back to the bedroom and dismantled the bed frame. The siderail that held the mattress was made of sturdy old iron. It was heavy, but together the two young women were able to carry it easily. They set it down a moment while Marie wiped the sweat off her face. Nancy tied up her hair in a high ponytail, then rubbed her sweaty palms against her jeans. She glanced down at her new blouse. It was covered with dirt from the filthy floor. She looked and felt a mess.

"The door is bolted, but before I came inside, I noticed the shutters just have a wooden bar across them. I think we can jar one loose and get out of here," Nancy suggested, testing the shutters one by one. Marie had already lifted all the windows and screens. "This shutter rattles a little already."

Standing close to the shuttered window, Nancy hoisted one end of the iron siderail, Marie the other. "On the count of three!" Nancy said as they began to swing the metal rod back and forth. "One. Two. *Three!*" The two young women shoved the improvised ramrod into the shutters. A satisfying sound of splintering wood filled the cabin. The shutter was damaged, but when Nancy tested it, it still wouldn't open.

"Another shot will do it," Nancy said, pausing with her hands on her ribs trying to catch her breath.

After a moment they tried again. This time the shutter exploded open, shards of wood flying outward. Nancy slapped Marie five. "We did it!" Then, grabbing her bag and her broken phone, Nancy followed Marie out the window, into the warm fresh air.

Of one mind, they both headed first to the outdoor water pump. Marie worked the pump while Nancy filled Marie's water bottle, then splashed cold water on her face and neck. Her blouse was soaked and possibly ruined, but the cool water revived her. After Marie drank some water, the girls found the red-marked trail back to the parking area.

Forty-five minutes later, by pushing the speed limit, Nancy reached the planetarium. The parking area was empty. Since it was Monday, the whole complex, including the science center, was closed to the public. A few cars dotted the far end of the front lot, but Nancy pulled around toward the back. If Jake and Bruce were up to no good, they wouldn't want their cars parked in full view of the main entrance and the road.

Nancy and Marie sat in the Mustang a moment longer surveying their surroundings. Two large green metal Dumpsters bordered the cow pasture behind the main building. In the distance the tin roof of McGinty's barn glinted in the afternoon sun. To the right of the Dumpsters stood a prefab storage shed. The door was open. Nancy could see lawnmowers, a snowplow attachment for a tractor, lots of spades, and other tools. No room for a captive in there, she realized, her heart sinking. Had they come to the wrong place?

"I still think we should have stopped and called the cops," Marie said nervously.

Nancy disagreed. "There was no time, Marie. Whoever you heard through the door back at the cabin, seemed in a rush to move Dr. Stars. And they had at least forty-five minutes to an hour's head start on us. If we lose him now, we might not be able to find him again."

"But have we found him?" Marie asked the same question that was troubling Nancy.

"Nancy, look over there, behind the Dumpsters," Marie suddenly said. She pointed just past the barbed-wire fencing in the pasture. Jutting from the weeds was the stone foundation of the old McGinty farmhouse that had burned down when Nancy was just a kid. Not far from the remains of the house, Nancy spied a large shed made of weathered wood, with a steeply banked black shingled roof. A row of tiny windows, glass panes broken, stretched along the side wall, high up, just under the sagging roof. It looked like an old chicken coop. The roof shingles were buckled, the weathered clapboard was in need of a paint job, but it was big enough for a couple of people to camp out in. A familiar tingling feeling shot down Nancy's spine. "This is the place! I'm sure of it!"

She jumped out of the car, careful to close the door quietly. Marie followed suit. After checking the inside of the tool shed, Nancy used the Dumpsters for cover as she crept up on the small wooden structure. As she peeked around the corner of the prefab shed, she gasped at the sight of a motorcycle parked at the edge of the planetarium lot, near the pasture fence. She turned on Marie, her eyes suspicious. "Marie—what's your motorcycle doing here?"

"My bike?" Marie repeated, shocked. She looked over Nancy's shoulder, and Nancy heard her sigh with relief. "That's not my bike. That's Bruce's. We both drive Harleys, but his is a different model!"

"I'm glad to hear that," Nancy said, reaching behind her and patting Marie's arm. So it could have been Bruce, not Marie, who had tried to run Bess down the other day outside Carson Drew's office.

Nancy had never pinned Bess down about seeing Marie's red hair, but now none of that mattered—except it made finding Dr. Stars even more urgent. If Bruce was willing to risk Bess's life just to scare her off, then what would he do to a man who could actually send him to jail? "I'll explain later" was all she told Marie now.

Surreptitiously they approached the electrified fence. "It's been cut!" Marie whispered.

"Now, why is *that* no surprise?" Nancy remarked wryly. She'd bet a million bucks that good old Bruce was handy with those wire cutters. "Just like the fence at Woody Acres," she added.

"It's awfully quiet," Marie observed. "Maybe they're not here?"

"Bruce's bike is. Let's move in closer." Nancy made herself small and slithered through the narrow opening in the fence, then turned to hold it for Marie. They walked softly along the long side wall of the shed, careful to keep their heads below the windows. Bees hummed around the wildflowers, and the scent of blossoms on the breeze almost masked the pasture smells of cows and manure. As they rounded the corner of the building, Nancy saw the door was open. Three cement blocks served as steps up to the rather high doorsill. Flies buzzed around a pail of garbage perched on the edge of one of the blocks.

Nancy crept up behind the door. Angry voices floated out from inside.

"Look, man, I'm not going to risk his talking!" someone snarled.

Marie tapped Nancy's shoulder. "That's Bruce," she whispered.

Nancy put a finger to her lips and leaned forward to listen.

"And I'm saying, we cut our losses and just split. This has already gone further than I ever intended," the second man declared. "I'm no murderer!"

15

Cooped In

Murderer!

At the word, Nancy and Marie exchanged a horrified glance. Nancy leaned close to Marie's ear. "I know that voice!" she whispered hoarsely. "It's Dr. Stars—"

Marie corrected her quickly. "You mean Jake McCurdy—the fake Dr. Stars. I'm afraid the real one is inside—and he's in pretty big trouble. What do we do?"

Nancy shook her head. "I want to hear more," she whispered.

Jake McCurdy sounded like a bundle of frayed nerves. His voice was pitched high. "Look, man. I only hired you to help me keep him under wraps for a couple of days. He wasn't supposed to get hurt. I'm not paid to take a rap for murder!"

"Yeah, well, kidnapping's a federal offense," another voice snarled.

Marie leaned over and murmured in Nancy's ear. "That's definitely Bruce!"

"Get real, Lankowski!" Jake fumed. "What if you killed that snoopy Drew girl back at the cabin?"

"I didn't kill anyone. But as for this guy—he's got to disappear for a while."

"But he knows who we are."

"I'm good at disappearing into the woodwork," Bruce told Jake. "Fake IDs are easy to come by."

"What about me?" Jake asked.

"Lay low for a while. This will all blow over," Bruce assured.

"And him?"

Nancy heard the sound of something being kicked, followed by a low moan. She winced. Her own question was answered. Dr. Stars was definitely inside—and alive, at least for the moment.

"Leave him here," Bruce suggested. "Maybe someone will find him before he croaks."

"No. That's still murder. Let me think, man." Nancy heard the sound of someone pacing. Suddenly the footsteps neared the door.

With a frantic gesture she motioned Marie to move back. The two girls ducked around the corner. Parting a clump of high weeds sprouting near the edge of the shed, Nancy watched as Jake stepped out onto the first cinder-block step and then stared out past the Dumpsters.

Nancy's heart leaped into her throat. What if he saw her car? But he was too absorbed in his own

132

thoughts to notice much of anything. "Wait here!" she told Marie, then crept back quietly toward the door.

Gathering her courage, Nancy craned her neck and glanced inside. As Nancy suspected, the place had been converted from a chicken coop to some kind of hangout—probably by some of the farmer's kids. Rock star and video game posters were tacked to the walls. A couple of milk crates, a tin-topped kitchen table, a decrepit futon mattress, and several oversize pillows provided the furnishings. On the table Nancy noticed some empty beer and soda cans, a half-eaten sandwich, and a cell phone.

From where Nancy stood, she could see Bruce. The guard was leaning on both hands on the table, profile to Nancy. The other man had his back to the door. In a chair, bound and gagged, sat a plump balding man. Exactly like his cartoon logo! Nancy realized. Definitely the real Dr. Stars. He was facing outward. His eyes widened slightly as he saw Nancy in the doorway, then he quickly averted his gaze.

Good! Though the man appeared to be stressed out, he was alert enough not to give her away.

Waving away a cloud of flies, Nancy stole back to Marie's side. She told her of the setup inside the shed. Then Marie nodded as Nancy shared her rescue plan.

While Marie went back to the door, Nancy circled the shed, coming around to the front from the other side.

Nancy burst inside the door, Marie right behind her.

"Hey, what the—" Bruce shouted as Nancy tackled him, throwing her whole weight onto him. As she had planned, the shock of seeing her had left him vulnerable to her attack.

Jake McCurdy pivoted on his heels and hurled himself outside and down the steps. Marie plunged out of the shed after him.

Meanwhile, Nancy was struggling with Bruce. He tried to pin her to the floor, but Nancy had wrenched his arm into an awkward position. He thrashed and kicked, struggling to shake her off. Though he was a slim, slightly built man, he had arms of steel. With a loud grunt and a burst of energy, he threw Nancy off and reached for her wrist. Nimbly Nancy leaped to her feet and neatly sidestepped him, her quick move sending him off balance. He stumbled but swiftly regained his footing.

"You little witch!" he snarled at Nancy. "You'll be sorry for this!" he roared. He kicked an electric lantern off the top of a plastic milk crate. Grabbing the crate, he hefted it into the air and aimed it down toward Nancy's head. She jumped, barely getting clear of the crate. The force of the gesture sent him lurching to one side.

Seizing the moment, Nancy lifted her arm high and brought her hand down in a powerful karate chop against his shoulder.

With a groan, he crumpled to the floor. Catching her breath, Nancy cast a quick glance at Dr. Stars. She realized he was all right for the moment. Nancy checked to see that Bruce was still half out of it, lying curled in the corner.

134

But what about Marie?

"I'll be right back!" she yelled over her shoulder as she raced for the door. Outside, Marie was holding Jake McCurdy with one arm. He was standing passively as she reached for her handcuffs.

"You okay?" she shouted to Nancy as she clamped the cuffs over Jake's wrists.

"Yeah, but Bruce isn't," Nancy told her.

Marie's eyebrows shot up. "Good job, Drew."

Marie led Jake back up the cement block steps into the shed. She sat him down on one of the crates, then tied Bruce up and propped him against the wall. He was conscious but groggy. She picked up the cell phone and dialed the police as Nancy freed Dr. Stars.

"Whoever you are," he gasped between grateful gulps of water, "I don't know how to thank you."

"We're just glad you're all right," Nancy said, then introduced herself and Marie as she helped him to stand up.

Nancy held his elbow as she made him slowly stretch. While he gingerly worked out the kinks in his legs and arms, she asked Dr. Stars what had happened.

"It's all a bit of a blur—I'm not even sure what day it is," the astronomer admitted, smoothing his hand over his bald head. "Let's see. I had just finished setting up for my lecture on Friday night."

"So it really was scheduled for Friday," Nancy interrupted, glaring at Jake.

"Anyway," the real Bob Steller continued, "I had put up my poster, and I was going back to the van to write in my notebook and e-mail my wife—" He broke off suddenly and grabbed Nancy's hand. "She must be worried sick. I never miss writing her."

"I know," Nancy said soothingly. "She's been posting messages on your Web site. When we get out of here you can e-mail her—"

"I can do it now," he said interrupting. "Jake took my laptop. It's somewhere in that pile of stuff." Dr. Stars motioned toward a duffel bag in the corner.

Nancy retrieved the laptop from one of the bags. Dr. Stars checked his battery power. It was low. "Can I borrow that cell phone?" He hooked up the cell phone to the laptop and logged on, sending a quick note to Teresa.

After he signed off and closed his laptop, Dr. Stars resumed his story. He was sitting inside his van with both front doors open as he made his daily journal entry. Suddenly he felt something jab him in the back. "That guy in the corner"—Dr. Stars gestured toward Bruce, who glowered back at him—"said he had a gun."

"A gun?" Nancy jumped up. "Where?"

"There's no gun," Bruce sneered. "There never was. I faked it with a stick. He fell for it, that's all."

Dr. Stars shot Bruce a withering look. "I was playing it safe. Anyway, I figured as long as I was conscious, I had some control over what might happen to me. I thought he and his buddy there were after my equipment. When they made me get out of the van and started marching me down that trail, I began to worry. Where were they taking me? It could be days before anyone found me, though I figured if I didn't turn up for the star watch that night, someone might alert the police."

136

Nancy explained about Jake's deception. Dr. Stars shook his head in disbelief. "No one reported me missing then? Amazing. But you're a good twenty years younger than me," he said to Jake.

"No one knows what you look like," Jake spoke up finally. "At least no one around here."

Dr. Stars sighed. "When I saw they were more or less kidnapping me, I tried to leave some sort of trail."

"What trail?" Bruce bellowed from the corner. He had straightened up and Nancy realized he was recovering.

"The one I followed," Nancy said with some satisfaction. "It started with the focusing knob. I spotted that first." She turned to Dr. Stars. "How did you manage to take it off the telescope and—"

Dr. Stars grinned sheepishly. "I didn't. I had lost the knob when I packed up after my last lecture up in Michigan. I bought a new one, but it was still in my pocket when these guys abducted me."

"It must have been hard for you to leave your ring as a clue," Nancy said, reaching in her pocket and handing it back to him.

"It was hard to get off, and even tougher to think I might never see it again. But I felt if I had any chance of being rescued it was worth losing the ring, if it meant seeing my wife again." A sad, tired expression crossed the astronomer's face. After a moment's silence he gathered himself together and resumed his tale. "Right after I dropped the ring, Bruce finally thought to blindfold me. I guess in case I escaped, and might remember the trail back to the campgrounds. When he took the blindfold off I wasn't sure where I was, exactly, but through the window in that room I could see some of the stars. By watching their progress through the night, I realized they hadn't moved me far. What I don't get is why kidnap me of all people?"

"Because you provided the perfect excuse for spying on another kind of star," Nancy pointed out. The astronomer still looked befuddled.

"They said something about taking pictures and selling them, but I never understood."

"Your Star Van tour was advertised well in advance," Marie told Dr. Stars. "Obviously Mr. McCurdy here was on to you. He must have researched the location of the day use area in the park as soon as he heard that Will Ryder's wedding was being held at Woody Acres."

"Your observing station overlooks the estate," Nancy pointed out.

The astronomer looked sadly at Jake. "I was right about you, then."

"How?" Jake asked warily.

"You really aren't a 'bad' guy—not like that one." Dr. Stars gestured toward Bruce. "Now, he's mean," the astronomer said, "but you're the scheming type. Too bad you can't put that mind to good use," he addressed Jake sharply. "What a waste! We had some pretty in-depth talks on astronomy."

"I wouldn't give him so much credit," Marie chimed in. "He probably wanted to pump you for information so he could do a better job pretending he was you," Marie charged.

"Not completely," Jake spoke up, his eyes sparking angrily. "I've always loved stargazing—"

Marie rolled her eyes. "Sure. Of the Hollywood kind."

"No, of the astronomy kind," Jake countered hotly. "I was in the astronomy club in high school and even took astronomy for my science requirement in college."

"So that explains it," Nancy broke in. "Why you knew a lot about some things, and nothing about other stuff. At the same time you did a pretty good job of wrecking Dr. Stars's reputation around here."

"What do you mean?" Bob Steller asked.

"He basically made 'Dr. Stars' sound like a fool—at least that's what the local astronomy buffs think. But when I tell Richard, who's active in the local astronomy club, what really happened, he'll set the record straight in the newsletter," Nancy assured the doctor. "But Jake made a mess of things, that's for sure."

"Yeah, I guess. I could tell people were on to me, and that's why I kept asking the old professor here to fill me in on more details."

"Speaking of details." Nancy approached Bruce. The guard looked up at her through narrowed eyes. "Tell me, was it you who tried to run over my friend Bess on Saturday outside the Protection and Detection offices?"

"For what it's worth," he growled, "yes. But I wasn't trying to run her over. I just wanted to scare her off Ryder. If she kept trailing him, she was sure to figure out what Jake and I were up to."

"And you're the only one who could have conned the park into turning on the lights because of that supposed prowler." Marie eyed Bruce with a mixture of disappointment and anger.

139

"The prowler wasn't 'supposed,' " Bruce shot back. He jerked his head toward Jake. "It was Jake, trying to video Ryder and Isabel hanging out around the estate before the wedding. Unfortunately I forgot to disarm the alarm Friday night, which alerted the cops."

At the sound of sirens in the distance, Marie cast a pitying look at Bruce. "How'd you rope him into this?" she asked Jake.

"Easy." Jake shrugged. "Money. He stood to gain some pretty big bucks plus a cushier job back at the TV station in L.A. that I had lined up to buy the story. I knew he couldn't hang around here after the story broke. You'd both probably be fired for not protecting precious Will Ryder and his bride," he told Marie.

Nancy stepped up to the door. Several state police cars had converged on the back lot of the planetarium. She waved toward the troopers. "They're in here!" she shouted. Spotting Trooper Caruso, she grinned. "I've caught your prowler," she told him as he approached the chicken coop.

The trooper looked into the shed. "We'll take over from here, but you young women should follow us down to the barracks to make a statement."

Nancy stepped aside to let the officers pass. A moment later they emerged with both Jake and Bruce. Jake was trying to explain that he needed to call his office.

"Shut up," Bruce admonished. "You'd better wait until you've got a good lawyer before you say a word." Nancy watched as the police trundled the two men down the concrete steps.

Bruce turned and met her eyes. "Speaking of good lawyers, I just happen to know one. Little Miss Snoop's dad. Maybe I'll call him."

Nancy's jaw dropped. The creep!

"Like he'd take on scum like you!" Marie exclaimed hotly.

16

Starlight, Starbright

"Be his lawyer?" Carson Drew exclaimed that evening as he leaned in the doorway of his study. "That guy's got some nerve. After he hit my daughter over the head."

"It was Bruce, then, who attacked you?" George asked Nancy. George and Bess had come over after dinner to hear all the details of Nancy's rescue of Dr. Stars, as well as to share the chocolate cake Hannah had baked for dessert. Dessert had turned into an impromptu celebration and gab fest.

Nancy nodded from over by the desk. She had logged on to the Internet to check the bulletin board on Dr. Stars's Web site, and maybe post a message of her own to clear his good name. "Jake spilled the beans down at the trooper barracks. He's hoping to plea out on the kidnapping charges."

"Can he get away with that?" Bess remarked, horrified.

"I doubt that'll wash. This is going to be a high-profile case," Mr. Drew said, straightening up and starting out the door. "I'm sure you girls have a lot to talk about."

George leaned over the back of Nancy's chair and peered at the monitor. "Hey, Nan, Dr. Stars's wife did get the message he sent from that shack today. Listen to this." George read aloud. "Glad to hear you're back from that black hole you fell into. Hope to hear details soon. Love, Teresa."

"That's so cool!" Bess remarked.

"Though I'd hate to see her face when she hears exactly what sort of black hole her husband fell into," Nancy said. "By the way, when we gave him a lift back to the Star Van, he gave me a copy of his most recent book, as a thank-you present."

"I'd love to see it," George remarked.

"It's in the study. You can borrow it. I think I've done enough stargazing for the moment," Nancy admitted.

Nancy turned off the computer, and the girls headed back into the family room. The half-demolished cake was on the table. A video of Bess's favorite Will Ryder flick—the one that won him an Oscar two years before—was playing on the TV.

Bess cut herself another sliver of cake, then flopped down next to Nancy on the comfortable brown sofa. "Now, this is heaven."

"I have to agree," George remarked. "Cake isn't usually my thing—unless it's baked by Hannah Gruen."

The doorbell chimed, interrupting the girls' laughter. They heard Hannah's voice calling from the hallway, "I'm coming, I'm coming," followed by the low murmur of voices.

"Probably someone to see Dad," Nancy guessed. "Bess, George, who wants the last slice?" She waved the cake knife in the air.

"Hey!" a deep friendly voice called from the door to the den. The three girls looked up. Nancy's eyes widened. Will Ryder was standing in the doorway. "Looks like we've crashed a party. Hope it's okay?" the movie star said, his lips curving up in his famous on-screen smile. Without taking her eyes off Will, Nancy quickly put down the knife and reached for the remote to flick off the TV.

Behind Will, Isabel Ramos-Garcia smiled broadly at the girls. Next to Isabel, Nancy spied Marie. "Uh— come on in," Nancy invited, casting a quick glance at Bess.

"It's okay?" Isabel asked.

"Okay? You've got to be kidding!" Bess practically shrieked. "It's great," she added in an almost normal tone after a sharp elbow poke from George.

"We've almost finished the cake Hannah just made, but there are chips and salsa," Nancy offered.

"Thanks, we've just eaten," Will said, his blue eyes twinkling. "You know the last meal before the execution."

Isabel pretended to pout. "So our marriage is now an execution?" she retorted in her light Spanish accent.

"Only kidding, honey." Will took Isabel's hand and held it tightly.

"We wanted to stop by to thank you personally for

all your help, Nancy. And you guys, too." Will nodded toward George and Bess.

"It was all Nancy—Nancy and Marie," George pointed out quickly.

"Whatever," Isabel said. "We so wanted a private, friends-and-family-only wedding. To think Jake Mc-Curdy almost blew it for us. You have no idea what a relief it is to know he's out of the picture."

"And will be for a long time," Marie said. Then she asked Nancy. "Did you ever find your wallet?"

Nancy nodded. "Jake had it in his duffel bag—I believed him when he said he just wanted to make it look like someone had mugged me for my credit cards and money. I've got it back. That's what matters."

"We're so grateful," Isabel spoke up, sharing a glance with Will. "And we wanted to bring this over in person, just to thank you guys."

Will dug into the shopping bag Marie handed to him. From its depths he retrieved a gaily wrapped package and put it in Bess's hands.

"For me?" For a second, Bess looked bewildered. Then she tore off the wrapping and opened the package. "You didn't have to," she said, glowing, as she pulled out a small camera. "I thought Protection and Detection was going to make good on this."

Will just shrugged. "Hey, they'd just bill my account anyway. Figured I'd do better getting it for you myself."

"It's a point-and-shoot," Isabel explained, "like the one that got broken."

Marie cast Bess an apologetic look. "My fault actually, but instead of my pay getting docked for it, Mr.

Ryder came to my rescue." Marie paused. "Bess, I am sorry I was so rough on you that day."

Bess blushed. "Actually, *I* should apologize." She turned to Will and Isabel. "I shouldn't have been spying on you."

"Hey, it's part of the territory. The fame thing," Will offered generously.

"It's a great camera," Bess said, "absolutely, the best, coming from you. . . ." Bess's blush deepened. Then she hugged Isabel and stood there looking sheepish. Isabel laughed and gave her a kindly shove in Will's direction, "Lucky I'm not the jealous type, Bess."

"You see how she disrespects me." Will laughed. "I love her for it." He gave Bess a big hug.

"That's it. She'll never be the same again," Nancy joked, shaking her head at Bess, who stood there looking dazed.

"And this is yours, Nancy." Will handed her her 35-millimeter camera. "I've put in some new film. You never know when it'll prove useful in catching another crook."

Isabel pointed at her wristwatch and Will took the cue. "We've got a wedding tomorrow, so we'd better hit the road."

"I'm riding back to the estate with them," Marie told Nancy. "I'm still on duty tonight, but let's keep in touch."

"I'd like that," Nancy said, giving Marie a quick hug.

Nancy and George walked them all to the limo parked at the foot of the driveway. "Where's Bess?" George asked under her breath. Nancy looked up to see Bess hurrying out of the house, Hannah Gruen in tow. Hannah was wiping her hands on a dish towel, and Bess was hurriedly explaining something to her.

"Wait up, everyone!" Bess cried as Will and Isabel started to climb into the backseat.

"I know this isn't official or anything, but please, just as a souvenir, could we take a picture of all of us together, with my new camera?"

Will shielded his face and mugged a horrified look. "What, another tabloid reporter in disguise?"

Bess's smile drooped. At the sight of Bess's dismal expression, Will chuckled. "Just kidding, Bess." With that he drew Bess up close to him, and slung one arm over her shoulder, the other over Isabel. Nancy, George, and Marie crowded close together.

"Just point and shoot, Hannah!" Bess instructed.

"Say cheese, everyone," Hannah instructed.

"Cheese!" six voices shouted in unison.

The flash went off and Bess cried out. "Now I'm really seeing stars!"

The Fascinating Story of One of the World's Most Celebrated Naturalists

Celebrating 40 years with the wild chimpanzees

MY LIFE with the CHIMPANZEES

by JANE GOODALL

From the time she was girl, Jane Goodall dreamed of a life spent working with animals. Finally, when she was twenty-six years old, she ventured into the forests of Africa to observe chimpanzees in the wild. On her expeditions she braved the dangers of the jungle and survived encounters with leopards and lions in the African bush. And she got to know an amazing group of wild chimpanzees—intelligent animals whose lives bear a surprising resemblance to our own.

Illustrated with photographs

A Byron Preiss Visual Publications, Inc. Book

2403

American S·I·S·T·E·R·S

Join different sets of sisters
as they embark on the varied,
sometimes dangerous,
always exciting journeys
across America's landscape!

West Along the Wagon Road, 1852

🙠

A *Titanic* Journey Across the Sea, 1912

🙠

Voyage to a Free Land, 1630

🙠

Adventure on the Wilderness Road, 1775

🙠

Crossing the Colorado Rockies, 1864

🙠

Down the Rio Grande, 1829

by Laurie Lawlor

2200-02

*Step back in time with Warren and Betsy
through the power of the Instant Commuter invention
and relive, in exciting detail, the greatest
natural disasters of all time...*

PEG KEHRET'S

THE VOLCANO DISASTER
Visit the great volcano eruption of Mount St. Helens
in Washington on May 18, 1980. . . .

THE BLIZZARD DISASTER
Try to survive the terrifying blizzard of
November 11, 1940 in Minnesota. . . .
Iowa's Children's Choice Award Master List

THE FLOOD DISASTER
Can they return to the Johnstown Flood
of May 31, 1889 in time to save lives?
Iowa Children's Choice Award Master List
Florida Sunshine State Award Master List

AND

THE SECRET JOURNEY
Twelve-year-old Emma Bolton is determined to join
her father and sick mother on the voyage to France.

3017